Praise for Ali Smith's

Public library and other stories

"A work of endless interventions. . . . Smith's greatest talent is her ability to produce on the page the effect of a human voice."

—Ian Samson, *The Guardian*

"An important book."

—*The Independent* (Books of the Year) (London)

"Superb. . . . [A] wonderful collection. . . . It has been Smith's unlikely triumph throughout her increasingly acclaimed career to combine a playful and experimental approach with material that is both moving and funny—and she has done it once again."

—*Daily Mail* (London)

"There are sentences that sing, or make you smile, and the conceit behind each of the stories is distinctively offbeat."

—*The Herald* (Glasgow)

"Spritely, poignant. . . . Magical. . . . Alive to the ability words have to garland a life and make the ordinary bloom into something fresh and funny." —*Mail on Sunday* (London)

"Reading this collection is like spending an afternoon in a well-stocked library in the company of an erudite and playful companion." —*The Daily Telegraph* (London)

"Smith's stories are so good as to be priceless."
—*Sunday Express* (London)

"Beautiful. . . . Wonderful. Her prose dances. Her imagination lights up life and experience. This is a book to read slowly, to savour its vitality and variety, one to return to and find new pleasures with each reading."
—*The Scotsman*

"Endearing and affecting. The extraordinary is always rooted in the corporeal . . . and this lends Smith's voice much of its considerable charm. . . . The narration is often arch, winking at you from the pages, rightfully proud of its own showmanship and subtlety, and is fundamentally human."
—*The London Magazine*

"A brilliant, comprehensive, unpredictable defence of public libraries. . . . You can travel anywhere on Ali Smith's library ticket."

—Kate Kellaway, *The Guardian*

"Powerful. . . . Beautifully written. . . . A gentle, comforting, and thought-provoking read. . . . It is a blessing to have authors such as Ali Smith." —*Stylist*

"Smith's world is incredibly generous—it's a place where all sorts of stories and human connections are possible." —*Metro* (London)

"A series of spirited short stories, in an ingenious blend of fact and fiction. . . . The result is a love song to literature that all readers will delight in dipping in and out of."

—Lucy Brooks, *Culture Whisper*

"[A] moving, surprising, beautiful collection. . . . So clever and so joyful."

—*Open Democracy*

Ali Smith

Public library and other stories

Ali Smith is the author of many works of fiction, including the novel *Hotel World*, which was shortlisted for both the Orange Prize and the Booker Prize and won the Encore Award and the Scottish Arts Council Book of the Year Award, and *The Accidental*, which won the Whitbread Award and was shortlisted for the Man Booker Prize and the Orange Prize. Her most recent novel, *How to be both*, was a Man Booker Prize finalist and winner of the Bailey Women's Prize, the Goldsmiths Prize, the Costa Novel Award, and the Saltire Literary Book of the Year Award. Born in Inverness, Scotland, Smith lives in Cambridge, England.

By the same author

Free Love and Other Stories
Like
Other stories and other stories
Hotel World
The whole story and other stories
The Accidental
Girl Meets Boy
The first person and other stories
There but for the
Artful
Shire
How to be both

Public library
and other stories

ali smith

Public library and other stories

ANCHOR BOOKS
A Division of Penguin Random House LLC
New York

FIRST ANCHOR BOOKS EDITION, OCTOBER 2016

Library of Congress Cataloging-in-Publication Data
Names: Smith, Ali, author.
Title: Public library and other stories / Ali Smith.
Description: New York : Anchor, 2016.
Identifiers: LLCN 2016021974 (print) | LCCN 2016026238 (ebook) | ISBN 9781101973042 (softcover) | ISBN 9781101973059 (e-book)
Subjects: LCSH: Books and reading—Fiction. | BISAC: FICTION / Short Stories (single author). | FICTION / Contemporary Women. | FICTION / Literary.
Classification: LLC PR6069.M4213 A6 2016 (print) | LCC PR6069.M4213 (ebook) | DDC 823/.914—dc23
LC record available at https://lccn.loc.gov/2016021974

Anchor Books Trade Paperback ISBN: 978-1-101-97304-2
eBook ISBN: 978-1-101-97305-9

www.anchorbooks.com

Printed in the United States of America
10 9 8 7 6 5 4 3 2 1

For Hazel Beamish
and for Sarah Wood

This same book in a stranger's hands, half-known.
Those readers, kindred spirits, almost friends.
You are in transition; you are on the threshold.
The library is the place that gets you. Pure gold.
Jackie Kay

O magic place it was – still open thank God.
Alexandra Harris

Contents

Here's a true story. Simon, my editor, and I had been meeting to talk about how to put together this book you're reading right now. We set off on a short walk across central London to his office to photocopy some stories I'd brought with me.

Just off Covent Garden we saw a building with the word LIBRARY above its doors.

It didn't look like a library. It looked like a fancy shop.

What do you think it is? Simon said.

Let's see, I said.

We crossed the road and went in.

Inside everything was painted black. There was a little vestibule and in it a woman was standing behind a high reception desk. She smiled a hello. Further in, straight ahead of us, I could just glimpse some people sitting at a table and we could hear from behind a thin partition wall the sounds of people drinking and talking.

Hello, we said. Is this a library?

The woman lost her smile.

No, she said.

A man came through from behind the partition. Hello, he said. Can I help at all?

We saw the word library, Simon said. Was this a library once? I said. She's a writer, Simon said by way of explaining. He's an editor, I said.

We're a private members' club, the man said. We also have a select number of hotel rooms.

I picked up a glossy leaflet from a pile on the desk about some kind of food promotion or taster deal. Simon picked up a card.

Have you actually got actual books? I said.

We do do some books as a feature. Please help yourself to a card, the man said a bit pointedly since we already had.

(Later, when I got home, I unfolded the advert I'd taken, which was for a company working with Library to produce three-course meals which allowed diners to relive your favourite musicals (Charlie and the Chocolate Factory | Phantom of the Opera | Les Misérables | Matilda)*. I typed in the Library website address off the advert. When it came up I noticed for the first time that a central part of the textual design of the use of the word Library was the thin line drawn through the middle of it: ~~Library~~.*

This is what ~~Library~~ listed next to the photographs of its 5 luxurious, individually designed, air-conditioned rooms with many modern amenities and comfortable beds: • Terrace Bar • 24 Hour Concierge • Ground floor lounge with stage and bar • Massage and Beauty treatment room • Kitchen with Chef's table (April 2015) • Private Dining and boardroom with conferencing • Double mezzanine with bridge • Smoking Terrace • Access to rare Library books.

Simon pocketed the card. I folded the advert about the food promotion into my inside pocket.

Thanks very much, we said.

Then we left.

We crossed the road and stopped on the pavement opposite, where we'd first seen the word above the door. We looked back at it. Simon shrugged.

Library, he said.

Now we know, I said.

*

In the UK over the past few years—over the length of time, in fact, that it's taken me to write these stories and edit this book—we've been having to fight hard to preserve an onslaught on our public library tradition. A series of politically driven public services cuts all over the country has been shredding away the rich and communal inheritance that this book in your hands—I could say any book in anyone's hands—celebrates.

When I published this collection in the UK it became part of a fierce fight, a growing national movement here determined to defend our public libraries. This happens to be a book that celebrates the communal impact on us of books and of reading, their vital importance when it comes to our individual lives and our shared histories—personal, cultural, social, local and international. It celebrates the ways our lives have been at least enhanced and at most enabled and transformed by access to public libraries.

Democracy of reading, democracy of space: our public library tradition, wherever we live in the wide world, was incredibly hard-won for us by the generations before us and ought to be protected, not just for ourselves but in the name of every generation after us.

Now here's the book, crossing the world like books do, and here's a greeting to the readers of this new North American edition. Hello. This book wishes you well. It wishes you the world. It wishes you somewhere warm, safe, well-lit, thoughtful, free, wide open to everybody, where you'll be surrounded by books and all the different possible ways of reading them. It wishes you fierceness and determination if anyone or anything threatens to take away your open access to place, space, time, thought, knowledge.

It wishes you libraries—endless public libraries.

Last

I had come to the conclusion. I had nothing more to say. I had looked in the cupboard and found it was bare. I had known in my bones it was over. I had reached the end of my tether. I had dug until I'd hit rock bottom. I had gone past the point of no return. I had come to the end of the line.

But at the end of the line, when the train stopped, like everybody else I got off and walked back along the platform to the exit. I scrabbled in my pocket for the ticket, fed the ticket into the slot in the machine. The machine snatched it with what felt like volition but what was really only automation, then opened its padded gates for me and shut them behind me. Then I walked out past the taxis, across the dismal car park and up the pedestrian bridge.

From here I could see the empty train, the same train we'd all just been on, as it shunted from the platform to wherever the empty trains go. From this angle I could see into the carriages, in fact I could see right into the carriage I'd just travelled to the end of the line in.

The carriage had been packed, all the seats taken ten minutes before the train left and the train still filling with people until the moment before its doors closed on us; the journey had been an exercise in aloofness, with people who didn't know each other swaying towards then carefully away from each other in the aisles, people trying to not sway into each other in the doorways, people towering above the rather buxom woman in the wheelchair, reading the magazine. She'd been there in the special wheelchair-designated place when I boarded the train. Somehow the swaying standing people were worse above her head, I thought, than they were above the heads of people just sitting ordinarily in the train seats; somehow it was the last word in rudeness, that the edge of one man's open jacket kept brushing against the back of her head.

That's how I knew, from up here on the slant of the bridge, that this train below was the same train I'd just been on, and that's how I could spot exactly the carriage I'd been on, because that woman in the wheelchair who'd been in the same carriage as me was still there on that empty train, I could see from here that she was leaning forward in her chair and beating on the train door with her fist. I could see she was yelling. I knew she was making a lot of noise and I knew I couldn't hear any of it.

I watched the silent beat of her. Then the train slid out of view.

The driver will find her, I thought. Surely they check to make sure their trains are empty. Surely people must fall asleep or be caught on trains like that all the time. Probably she has a mobile and has called people and let them know. It's even possible that she wants to be on that train, that she's meant to be on it, there, alone.

But through the scratchy perspex of the other side of the pedestrian bridge I could see that there was a footworn footpath going down towards the rails, the kind we used to make in the riverbanks and slopes of the fields when I was a child, the kind that people make in places where paths aren't supposed to be.

At the bottom of the path the barbed-wire fence that shut the station off from the public was splayed open the size of a big dog or a crouching adult. Next to this hole was a sign which said, in letters large enough for me to be able to read them from here, that trespassing was prohibited, that the only people allowed past this point were rail personnel. If we find you trespassing you will be fined.

I found I was thinking about the person, or people, who'd originally worded that sign. Had there been special meetings held to decide the wording? Did they, or he, or she, pause for a moment at all over find and fined?

And why, anyway, did the word fine mean a payment for doing something illegal at the same time as it meant everything from okay to really grand? And was it at all connected that the word grand could also mean a thousand pounds? Did that mean that notions of fineness and grandness, in their travelling etymologies, were often tied up with notions of money? I hadn't a clue. But I had an urge to look them up in a dictionary and see. It was the first urge to do such a thing I'd had in quite a while.

I turned round. I retraced my steps down the slant of the bridge and under the little barrier between the bridge and the grassy bank. I went down the path towards the hole in the bent-back fence. I slid myself through the space without catching my clothes on any of the sharp cut-open bits of it and I stood up straight again in the litter next to the bramble bushes. I glanced one way then the other along the set of rails in front of me. A train was up ahead of me. I wondered if it was the right train. There was something fine in it, just walking along a forbidden track, thinking pointlessly about words. Travelling etymologies, that was a good phrase. It would be a good name for a rock band. It would be a good social-anthropological name for a tribe of people who jumped rolling-stock and lived on it, sheltering under waterproofed tarpaulins when it rained, sitting when it was sunny on the footplate spaces, if that's what they were called, or lying stretched out on the tops of the cargoes of carriages; reprobates, meaningful dropouts, living a freer, more meaningful life than any of us others was able to choose. The Travelling Etymologies. It was a good idea, and now, background-murmuring through my head again, for the first time in ages, was a welcome sound, the sound of the long thin neverending-seeming rolling-stock of words, the sound of life and industry, word after word after word coupled to each other by tough little iron joists, travelling from the past through the present to the future like rolling stones that gather moss after all.

I mean, take a rich, full word like buxom, which was a word I knew the history of, since at another point in my life, in what felt like a life centuries earlier than this one now, I had liked words immensely and thought a lot about using them and about how they were used. At the beginning of its history buxom meant obedient, compliant, gracious. Then later in time it meant blithe, and lively, then a bit later still it started to mean overweight, because larger people are traditionally seen as blithe and cheery. Then it stopped being about both men and women and became only about women, in a revealing fusion of compliant, obedient, merry and big-breasted.

Or the word aloof, which was a shipping term, came from luff, the word for the command to distance your boat from something too dangerously close to it. Or the word clue, too, which came from the word for a ball of thread and the coinage of which was probably something to do with the big ball of string Theseus took into the labyrinth with him to mark his way out and defeat the Minotaur. Ariadne got it from Daedalus, the inventor, and she gave it to Theseus, with whom she was in love, and the ball of string saved his life and made him a hero. Then he abandoned her on Naxos island. She woke on the beach and she hadn't a clue where he'd gone till she saw the sails of his ship disappearing over the sea's horizon. Now that's what I call aloof. I was walking the outside length of a dark, dead, switched-off train. Words were stories in themselves. Stamina was another good one, whose root and path I couldn't remember wholly but knew was something to do with the length of a person's life, the length of the life-force allotted to each of us at birth. Strength and fragility both, something lasting and something fearfully delicate, held there in the one word, and there in front of me was the door with the woman in the wheelchair behind it, who, when she saw movement below her – I say below her because I was down on ground level, quite different from platform level and platform perspective, and could look in through the dark glass of the door and make out her ankles on the chair's fold-out footrests – knocked what she could reach of herself and her chair against the glass with such eagerness, force and determination that I knew properly for the first time exactly what the word stamina meant.

Hello! I shouted up.

I saw her mouth open and close. I looked high above my head at the buttons with which we usually open the doors of trains. They were unlit, as I expected.

I stood back in the grass so she could see me more clearly and I waved my arms about. I realized I could say anything to this person and she wouldn't be able to hear; I realized that unless she could lip-read she'd not know what I was saying. I could ask her what had happened to her, why and how she was in a wheelchair. I could recite the whole of Kubla Khan by Coleridge, or tell her all about Theseus and Ariadne, and she'd have to listen, while not listening at all, obviously. It had the makings of the perfect relationship. I could tell her endlessly, boringly, about words and how they meant and why they mattered, and what had happened in my life to make them not matter.

Instead, what I found myself talking about was the place where my father had his workshop when I was a child, and how it had been at the back of the railway, so that I had spent a lot of my holiday hours in the grassy banks alongside sets of rails much like where we were now.

It's been bulldozed, years ago, I said to the woman behind the glass doors. There's a furniture warehouse on it now, it's a shopping mall and a station car park where the old workshops were. It was a kind of nowhere, a nowhere before the new nowheres that shopping malls are now. It was quite a special place. The grass there was thick with clover, presumably it still is, if there's any grassy space there that still goes straight down to earth. Finding four-leafed clovers there was pretty mundane. We found five- and six- and seven-leafed clovers there too, and once an eight. I put what I found in a book. I've no idea which book. They must still be somewhere on the shelves in the house, folded flat in there with their ridged green leaves arranged so you could see how many. I wonder if I'd find any if I were to go home and look for them tonight. Needle in a haystack. Clover in a shut book.

When I finished speaking the woman behind the doors began saying something impatient-looking. But listening for what I couldn't hear had made my ears different. Now I could hear birds, air, the traffic in the distance. Then what I could hear most clearly was unexpected music.

Three boys were coming along the path I thought of as my path now, along the side of the train. One had a ghetto blaster. A black dog with his lead trailing on the ground was ahead of them, stopping to sniff the grass and stones, then loping off in front again when the boys got ahead instead. The dog saw me and stopped. The boys stopped. They were all in clothes that looked too big for them. The dog was streamlined in comparison, held in one neat piece by his skin. They backed up two or three steps as if they were all part of the same single body. Then they shrugged apart and came forward again, because I was no threat to anyone.

Trespassing's illegal, one of the boys said to me when they were close enough.

I said nothing. I pointed to the woman in the train.

She's got wheels, man, the smallest boy said to the others.

All three waved to the woman. She waved back. One boy held up a packet of cigarettes. The woman nodded and shouted the silent word yes. The boy with the ghetto blaster turned the volume off.

Can't hear you, he shouted.

The woman mouthed the word yes again, with finesse, as if very quietly. The boy with the cigarette packet opened the packet, took out two cigarettes and threw them both at the shut door. Somehow it was funnier because he threw two cigarettes, not just one. The woman held up her hand as if to say, wait a minute. She put her other hand in a bag on the side of the chair and took out an umbrella with a hooked handle. Then she backed her chair away from the door. She wheeled herself into the carriage, lined up the wheelchair next to the train seats and, using all the strength in her arms, she lifted and shifted herself from the wheelchair on to the seat. She got her breath back. She bent her head over the umbrella, lengthened the umbrella somehow, then she reached with the lengthened umbrella to hook open the little train window above her.

The boys cheered. I did too. Now we could hear the woman's voice through the open window. She said in a voice that was proper, rather upper middle class, that she wished she'd thought how to open that window earlier, and that she would love a cigarette, that she hadn't had a cigarette for over five years now, that she deserved one after today. She thanked the boys. She turned then and said a separate hello to me, as if we were all at a party she'd thrown and she was simply emphasizing how very pleased she was to see each and every one of us.

I saw you on the train looking so thoughtful, she said. Thank you for finding me.

The notion that I had been seen, and that from the outside I had at some unknowing point looked thoughtful, made me feel strange, better. The idea that I had found anything filled me with wonder. As the boys took turns trying to throw single cigarettes up in the air and through the open window, I felt myself become substantial. Now the boys were scrabbling about on the ground trying to find the fallen cigarettes, arguing about picking the cigarettes up off the ground and not crushing them. They shouted with happiness when one went through the high window and landed on the woman's lap. They argued about whose aim was truest, who would be best to throw the little red plastic lighter.

Inside the train the woman waved her hands to get their attention.

She tossed the cigarette up at her mouth and caught it the wrong way round, like a minor circus trick. The three boys shouted their admiration. She took the cigarette out of her mouth, put it the right way round, then got herself ready to catch the lighter, which she did, with one hand. She lit her cigarette. The tallest, the shyest of the three, tapped on the sealed window with the stick he was carrying and pointed it at the No Smoking logo. He blushed with pleasure at the way his friends laughed, the way the woman laughed behind the window, the way I was laughing too.

I stood directly under the open window and shouted up through it that I was off to find someone to unlock the train and let her out.

The smallest boy snorted a laugh.

Don't need to go nowhere, he said. We'll get your friend out.

All three boys stood back from the train carriage. The smallest scouted about for a pebble. The other two bent down and picked up large stones. The dog started to bark. It was almost immediately after they began throwing the stones at the side of the train that the men in the luminous waistcoats came running towards us.

Shortly after this the afternoon came to an end. We said our goodbyes. We went our different ways. I myself went back to the station and bought a ticket home. What was it you were telling me down there? the woman asked me when she'd finally got off the train, after they'd backed it to a platform, opened its doors, brought the sloping ramp they use to help people in wheelchairs to get on and off and allowed her to wheel herself out. There were many apologies from people in suits and uniforms. Well, that's the last time I take the train! is what she said, with some campness and a great deal of panache, when the doors finally automatically hissed open on her like the curtains of a strange tiny theatre. The people on the platform laughed politely. She didn't mean it, of course she didn't.

In Shakespeare, the word stone can also mean a mirror.

The word pebble has, in its time, also meant a

lens made of rock crystal and a sizeable amount of gunpowder.

The word mundane comes from *mundus*, the Latin word for the world.

At one time the word cheer seems to have meant the human face.

The word last is a very versatile word. Among other more unexpected things – like the piece of metal shaped like a foot which a cobbler uses to make shoes – it can mean both finality and continuance, it can mean the last time, and something a lot more lasting than that.

To conclude once meant to enclose.

To tell has at different times meant the following: to express in words, to narrate, to explain, to calculate, to count, to order, to give away secrets, to say goodbye.

To live in clover means to live luxuriously, in abundance.

For the past month or so, while I've been editing and readying this book, I've been asking the friends and the strangers I've chanced to meet or spend time with what they think about public libraries – about their history, their importance and the recent spate of closures. Here's a transcription of one of the earliest responses I had, from Sarah Wood:

> *This is what I think of when I think of school holidays, me and my friend Lisa cycling at full speed on our bikes and the route is always to the library.*
>
> *It started before the time they'd let us walk to school by ourselves. But for some reason we were allowed to do this. First it was the branch library. We were eight or nine years old and we went most days. We'd get out our books, cycle home and*

read them in the garden in one go. It was an independence thing for sure – we went, chose, borrowed, pedalled home, read what we'd got, then went back again, chose again, came home again and read. We'd throw our bikes down outside its doors – I remember that like it was a part of it, and that we didn't have any money, but that we didn't need money: here transaction was a whole other thing. There was a scheme where you got points for taking out books and when you'd reached a certain number of points the prize was that you got to help the librarian tidy up the shelves. We all wanted to do that. We read as much as we could so we could win that prize. The librarian was canny.

Then the new library was built, a terribly stylish five-storey building, a giant addition to the borough where we lived. A real frisson came off the place, it still does when I remember it opening. It was cleverly imagined, beautifully designed. Inside the children's library there was a sunken reading space that went down into the floor, a small-scale amphitheatre where we sat, citizens of thought, books open on our knees. Across from us there was a window into the place where adult readers could go and listen to records on a great big semicircular sofa – the librarian, momentarily transformed into DJ, would put the record on a turntable on the librarian's desk and the people listening would plug in a set of headphones behind them on the sofa to hear it, music for free.

Art too: this was also the floor where you could borrow paintings and prints; you could take home a work of art to make your own home as stylish and modern as the library. Downstairs was fiction. Above us were the study carrels where the older children did their homework and all the pupils from different schools met and hung out together. It was exciting. It was like the future would be. In fact I got my first Saturday job there, which was the first time I saw the amazing off-floor facilities they had, the modern stacks full of – well, everything.

I can't tell you what the opening of that library was like where we lived – it was an event. It was a really fantastic moment in my life, in our lives, a moment of real change. The brand new building brought with it the idea that our local history was important – that books were important, but also that we were too, and that where we lived was, that it had a heritage and a future that mattered. There was something very grounded about that beautiful new build. I'm pretty sure that's why we were allowed to go there, on our bikes by ourselves like we did, so long as we cycled on the pavement there and back and were careful about the traffic.

Good voice

There was a man who had two sons. And the younger of them said to his father, Father, give me the share of property that is coming to me.

Did you know about this? I say to my father. There was a German linguist who went round the prisoner of war camps in the First World War with a recording device, a big horn-like thing like on gramophones, making shellac recordings of all the British and Irish accents he could find.

Oh, the first war, my father says. Well, I wasn't born.

I know, I say. He interviewed hundreds of men, and what he'd do is, he'd ask them all to read a short passage from the Bible or say a couple of sentences or sing a song.

My father starts singing when he hears the word song. *Oh play to me Gypsy. That sweet serenade.*

He sings the first bit in a low voice then the next bit in a high voice. In both he's wildly out of tune.

Listen, I say. He made recordings that are incredibly important now because so many of the accents the men speak in have disappeared. Sometimes an accent would be significantly different, across even as little as the couple of miles between two places. And so many of those dialects have just gone. Died out.

Well girl that's life in't it? my father says.

He says it in his northern English accent still even though he himself is dead; I should make it clear here that my father's been dead for five years. We don't tend to talk much (not nearly as much as I do with my mother, who's been dead for a quarter of a century). I think this might be because my father, in his eighties when he went, left the world very cleanly, like a man who goes out one summer morning in just his shirt sleeves knowing he won't be needing a jacket that day.

I open my computer and get the page up where if you click on the links you can hear some of these recorded men. I play a couple of the prodigal son readings, the Aberdonian man and the man from somewhere in Yorkshire. The air round them cracks and hisses as loud as the dead men's voices, as if it's speaking too.

So I want to write this piece about the first war, I tell my father.

Silence.

And I want it to be about voice, not image, because everything's image these days and I have a feeling we're getting further and further away from human voices, and I was quite interested in maybe doing something about those recordings. But it looks like I can't find out much else about them unless I go to the British Library, I say.

Silence (because he thinks I'm being lazy, I can tell, and because he thinks what I'm about to do next is really lazy too).

I do it anyway. I type the words First World War into an online search and go to Images, to see what comes up at random. *Austrians executing Serbs 1917. JPG. Description: English: World War I execution squad. Original caption: 'Austria's Atrocities. Blindfolded and in a kneeling position, patriotic Jugo-Slavs in Serbia near the Austrian lines were arranged in a semi-circle and ruthlessly shot at a command.' Photo by Underwood and Underwood. (War Dept.) EXACT DATE SHOT UNKNOWN NARA FILE: 165-WW-179A-8 WAR & CONFLICT BOOK no. 691 (Released to Public).* There's a row of uniformed men standing in a kind of choreographed curve, a bit like a curve of dancers in a Busby Berkeley number. They're holding their rifles three feet, maybe less, away from another curved row of men facing them, kneeling, blindfolded, white things over their eyes, their arms bound behind their backs. The odd thing is, the men with the rifles are all standing between two railway tracks, also curving, and they stretch away out of the picture, men and rails like it might be for miles.

It resembles the famous Goya picture. But it also looks modern because of those tracks.

There's a white cloud of dust near the centre of the photo because some of these kneeling men are actually in the process of being shot as the photo's being taken *(EXACT DATE SHOT)*. And then there are the pointed spikes hammered in the ground in front of every one of the kneeling prisoners. So that when you topple the spike will go through you too, in case you're not dead enough after the bullet.

Was never a one for musicals, me, my father says.

What? I say.

Never did like, ah, what's his name, either. Weasly little man.

Astaire, I say.

Aye, him, he says.

You're completely wrong, I say. Fred Astaire was a superb dancer. (This is an argument we've had many times.) One of the best dancers of the twentieth century.

My father ignores me and starts singing about caravans and gypsies again. *I'll be your vagabond*, he sings. *Just for tonight*.

I look at the line of men with the rifles aimed. It's just another random image. I'm looking at it and I'm feeling nothing. If I look at it much longer something in my brain will close over and may never open again.

Anyway, you know all about it already, my father says. You don't need me. You did it years ago, at the High School.

Did what? I say.

First World War, he says.

So I did, I say. I'd forgotten.

Do you remember the nightmares you had? he says.

No, I say.

With the giant man made of mud in them, the man much bigger than the earth?

No, I say.

It's when you were anti-nuclear, he says. Remember? There was all the nuclear stuff leaking on to the beach in Caithness. Oh, you were very up in arms. And you were doing the war, same time.

I don't. I don't remember that at all.

What I remember is that we were taught history by a small, sharp man who was really clever, we knew he'd got a first at a university, and he kept making a joke none of us understood, *Lloyd George knew my father* he kept saying, and we all laughed when he did though we'd no idea why. That year was First World War, Irish Famine and

Russian Revolution; next year was Irish Home Rule and Italian and German Unifications, and the books we studied were full of grainy photographs of piles of corpses whatever the subject.

One day a small girl came in and gave Mr MacDonald a slip of paper saying Please sir, she's wanted at the office, and he announced to the class the name of one of our classmates: Carolyn Stead. We all looked at each other and the whisper went round the class: Carolyn's dead! Carolyn's dead!

Ha ha! my father says.

We thought we were hilarious, with our books open at pages like the one with the moustachioed soldiers black as miners relaxing in their open-necked uniforms round the cooking pot in the mud that glistened in petrified sea-waves above their heads. Mr MacDonald had been telling us about how men would be having their soup or stew and would dip the serving spoon in and out would come a horse hoof or a boot with a foot still in it. We learned about the arms race. We learned about dreadnoughts. Meanwhile some German exchange students arrived, from a girls' school in Augsburg.

Oh they were right nice girls, the German girls, my father says.

I remember not liking my exchange student at all. She had a coat made of rabbit hair that moulted over everything it touched and a habit of picking her nose. But I don't tell him that. I tell him, instead, something I was too ashamed to say to him or my mother out loud at the time, about how one of the nights we were walking home from school with our exchange partners a bunch of boys followed us shouting the word Nazi and doing Hitler salutes. The Augsburg girls were nonplussed. They were all in terrible shock anyway, because the TV series called Holocaust had aired in Germany for the first time just before they came. I remember them trying to talk about it. All they could do was open their mouths and their eyes wide and shake their heads.

My father'd been in that war, in the Navy. He never spoke about it either though sometimes he still had nightmares, *leave your father, he had a bad night*, our mother would say (she'd been in it too, joined the WAAF in 1945 as soon as she was old enough). My brothers and sisters and I knew that his own father had been in the First World War, had been gassed, had survived, had come back ill and had died young, which was why our father had had to leave school at thirteen.

He was a nice man, poor man, he said once when I asked him about his father. *He wasn't well. His lungs were bad.* When he died himself, in 2009, my brother unearthed a lot of old photographs in his house. One is of thirty men all standing, sitting and lying on patchy grass round a set of WWI tents. Some are in dark uniform, the others are in thick white trousers and jackets and one man's got a Red Cross badge on both his arms. They're all arranged round a sign saying SHAVING AND CUTTING TENT next to a man in a chair, his head tipped back and his chin covered in foam. There's a list of names on the back. The man on the grass third from the left is apparently my grandfather.

We'd never even seen a picture of him till then. One day in the 1950s, after she'd been married to my father for several years, a stranger knocked at the door and my mother opened it and the stranger said my father's name and asked did he live here and my mother said yes, and the stranger said, who are you? and my mother said, I'm his wife, who are you? and the stranger said, pleased to meet you, I'm his brother. My father said almost nothing when it came to the past. My mother the same. The past was past. After my mother died, and when the Second World War was on TV all the time in anniversary after anniversary (fifty years since the start, fifty years since the end, sixty years since the start, sixty years since the end), he began to tell us one or two things that had happened to him, like about the men who were parachuted in for the invasion of Sicily but by mistake had been dropped too far out from land so the sea was full of them, their heads in the water and the ships couldn't stop, *you couldn't just stop a warship, we waved to them, we called down to them, we told them we'd be back for them, but we knew we wouldn't and so did they.*

Now I tell my father, who's five years dead,

you know, I wrote to the Imperial War Museum recently about that old picture with your dad in it, and I asked them whether the white clothes he's wearing meant anything special, a hospital worker or something, and a man wrote back and told me maybe your dad was an army baker but that to know for sure we'd need service records and that the problem with that is that 60% of First World War Army Records were burned in a German raid in 1940.

Things get lost all the time, girl, he says.

Do you know if he was a baker, maybe? I say.

Silence.

My grandfather doesn't look much like my father in the picture, but he looks a bit like one of my brothers. I've no idea what he saw in his war. God knows. There's no way of knowing. I'll never know what his voice sounded like. I suppose it must have sounded a bit like my father's. I suppose his voice was in my father's head much like my father's is in mine. I wonder if he could sing. *Red sails in the sunset*, my father sings right now, out of tune (or maybe to his own tune). *Way out on the sea*. Gas! – GAS! – quick, boys! –. That was the Wilfred Owen poem. In it gas was written first in small letters then in capitals, which, when I was at school, I'd thought very clever, because of the way the realization that the gas was coming, or maybe the shouts about it, got louder the nearer it came. *Oh carry my loved one. Home safely to me.* And Owen had convalesced, and met his friend Siegfried Sassoon, and learned to write a whole other kind of poetry from his early rather purple sonnets, at Craiglockhart Hospital near Edinburgh, which was close to home, even though Edinburgh was itself a far country to me, at fifteen, in Inverness, when I first read Owen. *He sailed at the dawning. All day I've been blue.*

My father's voice is incredibly loud, so loud that I'm finding it hard to think anything about anything. I try to concentrate. There was a thing I read recently, a tiny paragraph in the International New York Times, about a rare kind of fungus found nowhere else in the UK, but discovered growing in the grounds of Craiglockhart and believed by experts to have been brought there from mainland Europe on the boots of the convalescing soldiers. Microscopic spores on those boots and decades later the life. But I can't even think about that because *Red sails in the sunset. I'm trusting in you.* Okay.

I sing back, quite loud too, a song of my own choice. *War is stupid. And people are stupid.*

Don't think much of your words, my father says. Or your tune. That's not a song. Who in God's name sang that?

Boy George, I say. Culture Club.

Boy George. God help us, my father says.

The 1984 version of Wilfred Owen, I say.

Hardly, he says. Boy George never saw a war. Christ. What a war would've done to him.

Wilfred Owen was gay too, you know, I say.

I say it because I know it will annoy him. But he doesn't take the bait. Instead:

People aren't stupid. It's that song that's stupid, he says.

It's not a stupid song, I say.

You got that Wilfred Owen book as a school prize, he says.

Oh yes, so I did, I say.

You chose it yourself at Melvens, he says. 1st prize for German. 1978.

How do you remember all this stuff? I say. And really. What does it matter, what prize I ever got for anything?

You were good at German, he says. Should've kept on with your languages. Should've learned them all while you had the chance, girl. You still could. I wish I'd had the chance. You listening to me?

No.

No, cause you never listen, he says. And you were learning Greek last year –

How do you even *know* that? You're supposed to be dead, I say.

– and gave it up, didn't you? he says. As soon as it got too difficult.

The past and the future were hard, I say.

Start it again, he says in my ear.

Can't afford it, I say.

Yes you can, he says. It's worth it. And you don't know the first thing about what it means not to afford something.

I'm too old, I say.

Learn anything, any age, he says. Don't be stupid. Don't waste it.

While I'm trying to think of other songs I can sing so I don't have to listen to him (Broken English? Marianne Faithfull? *It's just an old war. It's not my reality)* –

here, lass, he says. Culture Club!

What about them? I say.

That fungus! In that hospital, he says. Ha ha!

Oh – ha! I say.

And you could write your war thing, he says, couldn't you, about when you were the voice captain.

When I was the what? I say.

And you had to lay the wreath at the Memorial. With that boy who was the piper at your school. The voice captain for the boys. Lived out at Kiltarlity. His dad was the policeman.

Oh, *vice* captain, I say.

Aye, well. Vice, voice. You got to be it and that's the whole point, he says. Write about that.

No, I say.

Well don't then, he says.

It was a bitter cold Sunday, wet and misty, dismal, dreich, everything as dripping and grey as only Inverness in November can be; we stood at the Memorial by the river in our uniforms with the Provost and his wife and some people from the council and the British Legion, and we each stepped forward in turn below the names carved on it to do this thing, the weight of which, the meaning and resonance of which, I didn't really understand, though I'd thought I knew all about war and the wars, until I got home after it and my parents, with a kindness that was quiet and serious, sat me down in the warm back room, made me a mug of hot chocolate then sat there with me in a silence, not a companionable silence, more mindful than that. Assiduous.

Damn. Look at that. I just wrote about it even though I was trying not to.

Silence,

silence,

silence.

Good. It's a relief.

That image of the soldiers on the railway tracks is still on the screen of my computer. I click off it and look up some pictures of Inverness War Memorial instead. Red sandstone, I'd forgotten how very red. I never knew before, either, that this

Memorial was unveiled in winter, 1922, in front of a crowd of five thousand. Imagine the riverbanks, the crowd. I'm pretty sure I never knew either till now, and it's a shock to, that one in every seven men from Inverness who fought in the First World War died, or that the Scottish Highlands had the highest casualty rate, per capita, of the whole of Europe. Then from God knows where my father says:

and do you remember, girl, when we drove around all that Sunday for the project you were doing at university, and you needed to record people speaking for it, but no one would stop and speak to you?

Yes! I say. Ha ha! It was for a linguistics class. I'd wanted to test out something I'd been told all through my growing up, that the people in and around Inverness spoke the best English. I'd made him ferry me round the town and all the villages between Ardersier and Beauly, trying to stop random people and get them to speak sentences into a tape recorder so I could measure the pureness of their vowels. For a start it was a Sunday, so there was no one much out and about. *But you know why it's called the best English*, one of the three passers-by who did stop when I asked said into the microphone. *It's because of the Jacobite wars with the English, because in the late 1700s when they banned the Gaelic – which was all anybody spoke here – and they moved the troops into Fort George and Fort Augustus and the soldiers intermarried with all the local girls, then the English that got spoken was a Gaelic-inflected English.*

Inflected, my father says now as if he's turning the word over in his mouth.

War-inflected.

That's it. I have a clever idea.

I go to the shelf and take down my Penguin Book of First World War Poetry. Its spine is broken and pages 187–208 are falling out of it.

I take a blank page and a pencil. I flick through the book and I make a list of everything I've happened to underline in it over the years.

Consciousness : in that rich earth : for the last time : a jolting lump : feet that trod him down : the eyeless dead : posturing giants : an officer came blundering : gasping and bawling : you make us shells : very real : silent : salient : nervous : snow-dazed : sun-dozed : became a lump of stench, a clot of meat : blood-shod : gas shells dropping softly behind : ecstasy of fumbling : you too : children : the holy glimmers of goodbyes : waiting for dark : voices of boys rang saddening like a hymn : a god in kilts : God through mud : I have perceived much beauty : hell : hell : alleys cobbled with their brothers : the philosophy : I'm blind : pennies on my eyes: piteous recognition : the pity war distilled : I try not to remember these things now : people in whose voice real feeling rings : end of the world : less chanced than you for life : oaths Godhead might shrink at, but not the lice : many crowns of thorns : emptied of God-ancestralled essences : the great sunk silences : roots in the black blood : titan : power : in thirteen days I'll probably be dead : memories that make only a single memory : I hear you still : soldiers who sing these days.

I read it. A man of mud and sadness rises like a great wave. He is like a great cloud much bigger than the earth, like an animation from a Ministry of Information film, amateur, jerky, terrifying. He is made of spores, bones, stone, feet still in their boots, dead horses, steel. He speaks with all the gone voices. He is a roaring silence. There are slices of railway track sticking out of his thighs and wrists.

I'm in tears. Christ.

The men in that picture were shooting people so close to them that they could have reached forward and touched them without even moving their feet, and the dust simply rose in the air as the people got shot.

My father jogs my elbow.

Come on, girl, he says.

He sings the song as loud as he can in his Gracie Fields falsetto.

Sticking out my chest, hopin' for the best.

He waits for me to sing.

War is stupid, I sing again.

He nods.

Wish me luck as you wave me goodbye, he sings. *Cheerio, here I go, on my way.*

He waves. I wave.

Say it in broken English, I sing back.

Kensal Rise Library, built by public subscription on a site donated by All Souls College, Oxford, was ceremoniously opened by Mark Twain in the year 1900.

It was closed by Brent Council in 2011 and sold to a property developer called Platinum Revolver.

Public pressure to save and protect the library has been so strong over the past four years that the property restorers now working on the site converting the space into flats (Uplift Property, whose marketing hook is 'homes to make you happy') have been forced to produce redevelopment blueprints which include both designated public space and designated library space.

This is what Pat Hunter told me:

Libraries have been a focal point in my life and work for seventy-five years. In my childhood (born 1932) one could only be enrolled at the library at seven years of age. In 1939 I did so with a sense of great awe and excitement. In 1949, at seventeen years, I went from sixth-form grammar school to work and train as a librarian, and finally retired in 1996 after forty years' service. In all those years I saw the value of and need for libraries to all the population.

The importance of libraries was recognized by the Public Libraries Act 1850 and affirmed by the Public Libraries and Museums Act 1964. In all the media mention of cuts to services in libraries I heard no reference to these Acts or any other statutory requirement for the provision of libraries – nor have they been rescinded.

Because libraries have always been a part of any civilization they are not negotiable. They are part of our inheritance.

The beholder

I had been having difficulty breathing so I went to the doctor. He couldn't find anything wrong. My respiratory function tests came out clear and strong. My heart was fine, my blood was fine. My colour was fine.

Tell me again, about the breathing, he said.

It starts slight, then gets sorer and sorer, I said. It's sore at the very top of my breath then sore at the very bottom of my breath. It feels like I've been winded. It's very unpredictable. I never know when it'll come or when it's going to go.

The doctor looked again at his computer screen. He clicked his tongue.

And life generally? he asked. How's life?

Fine, I said.

Nothing out of the ordinary? he said.

No, I said, not really, well, my dad died and my

siblings went mad and we've all stopped speaking to each other and my ex-partner is suing me for half the value of everything I own and I got made redundant and about a month ago my next-door neighbour bought a drum kit, but other than that, just, you know, the usual.

The doctor printed something out and signed it then handed it to me.

Take these, he said. Come back in a few weeks if life hasn't improved.

I went to Superdrug and they gave me a little box. In it was a blisterpack, three months' worth of antidepressant. I read the piece of paper that came with the blisterpack. It said that one of the side-effects was that these antidepressants would make you depressed. I left the pills unopened on the shelf in the bathroom. The pain came and went. When it came I sat very still, if I could, and tried not to think of anything. But it's hard not to think of anything. I often ended up thinking of something.

I thought of us going through the old clothes in a wardrobe in his house and outside all the apples in the grass going soft, just falling off his trees because none of us had thought to pick them. I thought of the liquidizer on the sideboard in the kitchen back when we were married, a thing which we simply used, in the days when things were simple, to make soup. I thought of the sheen on the surfaces of the tables all pushed together in the meeting room and the way that when I came back to my desk nobody, not even the people I had thought were my friends, would look at me. I thought of sleep, how much I missed sleep. I thought how it was something I had never imagined about myself, that one day I would end up half in love with easeful sleep.

Yes, see that? the unexpected word easeful just slipping itself in like into a warm clean bed next to the word sleep. Easeful. It wasn't a straightforward word, the kind of word you hear much or hear people use often; it wasn't an easeful word. But when I turned it over on my tongue even something about its sound was easeful.

Then one day not long after I had surprised myself by crying about, of all things, how beautiful a word can be, I had just got up, run myself a bath and was about to step into it. I opened the top buttons of my pyjamas and that's when I first saw it in the mirror, down from the collarbone. It was woody, dark browny greeny, sort of circular, ridged a bit like bark, about the size of a two pence piece.

I poked it. I stared at it in the mirror. I got the mirror down off the shelf and held it to my chest against myself.

I've no idea, the doctor said. I've never seen anything like it. It's definitely not a wart. I'm pretty sure it's not a tumour, at least it's nothing like any tumour I've seen.

He picked a pencil up off his desk. He sharpened

the pencil. He poked me with the blunt end of the pencil and then the sharp end.

Ow, I said.

And it hasn't changed since you first noticed it? he said.

No, I said, apart from that it's got a bit bigger, and then these four little stubby branch things, well, they're new.

He left me in the room with the obligatory nurse and came back with two of the other doctors from the practice, the old one who's been there since the surgery opened and the newest youngest one, fresh from medical school. This new young doctor filmed my chest on her iPhone. The most senior doctor talked her through filing a little of the barky stuff into one sterilized tube then another. Then the most senior doctor and my own doctor each fingered the stubs until my doctor yelped. He held up his finger. At its tip was a perfect, round, very red drop of blood. While all three doctors ran round the room ripping open antiseptic packaging, the nurse, who'd been sitting against the wall by the screen, gently tested with the tip of her thumb the point of one of the thorny spikes on the stub furthest away from my chest.

Really remarkably sharp, she said quietly to me. Have they nicked you at all in the skin?

Once or twice, I said.

Does it hurt when they do that? she said.

Hardly, I said. Not on any real scale of hurt.

She nodded. I buttoned my shirt up again carefully over the stubs. That week I had ruined three shirts. I was running out of shirts.

The young and the old doctor left. The nurse winked at me and left. My own doctor sat down at his desk. He typed something into his computer with difficulty because of the size of the bandage on his finger.

I'm referring you to a consultant, he said. Actually – you might want to make a note – I'm going to refer you to several consultants at the following clinics: Oncology Ontology Dermatology Neurology Urology Etymology Impology Expology Infomology Menthololology Ornithology and Apology, did you get all that? and when you see Dr Mathieson at Tautology, well, not to put too fine a point on it, he's the best in the country. He'll cut it straight out. You'll have no more problems. You should hear in the next ten days or so. Meanwhile, any discomfort, don't hesitate.

I thanked him, arranged my scarf over the bits of the stubs that were too visible through my shirt and left the surgery.

On my way to buy a new shirt, I met a gypsy. She was selling lucky white heather. She held out a sprig to me.

I'm sorry, I've no money, I said.

Well, she said looking me up and down, you've

not got much, true enough, I can see that. But you've a kind face, so money's the least of your worries. Give me everything you've got in your pockets and that'll be more than enough for me.

I had two ten pound notes in my purse and a little loose change in one of my pockets. I gave her the change.

Ah but what about those notes? she said. I can see them in your wallet, you know.

Can you? I said.

Burning a hole in you, she said.

If I give you all my money I'll be broke, I said.

Yes, you will, she said.

She held out the heather. I took it. It was wrapped at the stem in a little crush of tinfoil warm from her hand. She took my money and she tucked it into her clothes. Then she stood in front of me with her hands up in benison and she said:

may the road rise to meet you, may the wind always be at your back, may the sun shine warm upon your face, may the rains fall soft upon your fields, and until we meet again may absence make your heart grow, and I think that may well be a very nice specimen you've got there in your chest, if I'm not wrong, a young licitness.

A young what? I said but a couple of community police officers were strolling up the street towards us and she was busy tucking away her sprigs of heather into her many coat pockets, in fact it looked like her coat was more pocket than coat.

Give it a few hours of sun every day if you can, she called back over her shoulder as she went, stay well hydrated and just occasionally you'll need to add some good well-rotted manure and cut yourself back hard, but always cut on the slant, my lovely. All the best, now.

What did you say it was, again? I called.

But she was well gone; it wasn't until a bit later when I chanced to be whiling away an early spring afternoon wandering around in the park that I saw what I was looking for and found the right words for it. Meanwhile the letters from the clinics arrived, the first, then another, then another, then another, and as they came through the letterbox I piled them unopened on the hall table. Meanwhile the pairs of little stubby antlers grew and greened and notched themselves then split and grew again, long and slender, as high as my eyes, so that putting on a jumper took ten very careful minutes and I began to do a lot of improvisation with cardigans and V-neck vest-tops. There were elegant single buds at the ends of thin lone stems closed tight on themselves, and a large number of clustered tight-shut buds on some of the stronger thicker branches. My phone went off in my pocket and as I reached in, took it out, pressed Answer, arched my arm past the worst of the thorns and got the phone to my ear pretty much unscratched, the whole rich tangled mass of me swung and shifted and shivered every serrated edge of its hundreds and hundreds of perfect green new leaves.

Hello, a cheery voice said. I'm just doing a follow-up call after your visit and your tests earlier this month, so if you could just let us know whether there've been any changes or developments in your condition.

Yes, I said, a very important development, I know what it is now, it's called a Young Lycidas, it's a David Austin variety, very hardy, good repeater, strong in fragrance, quite a recent breed, I was in Regent's Park a couple of days ago and I saw it there, exactly the same specimen, I wrote down what the label said and when I got home I looked it up, apparently they named it only a couple of years ago after the hero of Milton's elegy about the shepherd who's a tremendous musician but who gets drowned at sea at a tragically young age.

Em –, the voice said.

Then there was a pause.

The other thing about Milton, I said, is that he was a great maker-up of words, and one of the reasons they named a rose after him, not just because it was an anniversary of his birth or death, I can't remember which, in 2008, is that he's actually the person who invented, just made up, out of nothing, the word fragrance. Well, not out of nothing, from a Latin root, but you know what I mean.

I waited but nobody spoke, so I went on.

And gloom, I said. And lovelorn, and even the word padlock we wouldn't have, if it wasn't for him just making it up. I wonder what we'd call padlocks if we didn't call them padlocks.

Then the voice began saying something serious-sounding about something. But I wasn't listening, I had seen a bird above the green of me, a swift, I saw it soar high in the air with its wings arched and I remembered as if I were actually seeing it happen again in front of my eyes something from back when we were first married, on holiday in Greece having breakfast one morning in our hotel.

It's a warm windy morning, it must be very windy because the force of the wind has grounded a swift, the kind of bird that's never supposed to land, a young one, still small. In a moment you're up on your feet, you drop your knife against your plate, cross the courtyard and scoop the bird up in both hands; it struggles back against you and a couple of times nearly wings itself free, but you cup it gently back in again, its head surprisingly grey and its eyes like black beads in the cup of your hands; I have never seen and am unlikely ever again to see a swift so clearly or so close. You carry it up the several flights of stairs till we get to the open-air roof of the building, you go to the very edge of the roof with it and then I see you throw your arms up and fling the bird into the air.

For a moment it rose, it opened its wings and held the wind. But then it fell, it was too young, the wind was still too strong for it. We ran down all those stairs as fast as we could and went out into the street to look for it, we looked all up and down the street directly below, but we couldn't find it. So God knows whether it made it. God knows whether it didn't.

Hello? the voice was saying more and more insistent, more and more officious in my ear, hello? but I was looking open-mouthed at the first burst of colour, a coiled whorl of deep pink inches away from my eyes, rich and layered petal after petal in the unfold of petal.

The scent was, yes, of roses, and look, four new buds round this opened flower had appeared too, I'd not noticed them till now and they looked as if they were really ready to open, about to any minute.

Yes, I said into the phone. Sorry. Hello.

Urgency, update, condition? the voice said.

Fine, I said. Life's fine. Life has definitely improved.

Yes, but. Results, hospital, inconclusive, the voice said. Urgent, immediate, straight away.

The voice had become implacable.

Surgery policy, the voice said.

Then it softened.

Here, it said. Help.

Well, I said, for now I'm okay though at some point soon I might need a bit of a hand with some trellising.

With –? the voice said.

I'm so sorry, I said, but I'm on a train and we may lose reception any mo –

I pressed the End Call button then switched my phone off because all four of those new buds had opened right before my eyes and I was annoyed that because I had been talking on a phone I had not seen a single one of them do it.

I have never yet managed to see the moment of the petals of a bud unfurling. I might dedicate the rest of my life to it and might still never see it. No, not might, will: I will dedicate the rest of my life, in which I walk forward into this blossoming. When there's no blossom I will dead-head and wait. It'll be back. That's the nature of things.

As it is, I am careful when kissing, or when taking anyone in my arms. I warn them about the thorns. I treat myself with care. I guard against pests and frost-damage. I am careful with my roots. I know they need depth and darkness, and any shit that comes my way I know exactly what to do with. I'm composed when it comes to compost.

Here's my father, a week before he died. He's in the hospital bed, hardly conscious. Don't wake me, he says, whatever you do. He turns over away from us, his back to us. Then he reaches down into the bed as if he's adjusting one of the tubes that go in and out of him and, as if there's nobody here but him – can he really be – the only word for it isn't an easeful word, it's the word wanking. Whatever he's doing under the covers for those few seconds he takes, it makes the word wank beautiful. He's dying. Death can wait.

A branch breaks into flower at the right-hand side of my forehead with a vigour that makes me proud.

Here we all are, small, on the back seat, our father driving, we're on holiday. There's a cassette playing: The Spinners; they're a folk band from TV, they do songs from all over the world. They do a song about a mongoose and a song about the aeroplane that crashed with the Manchester United team on board the time a lot of them died. That's a modern ballad, our father has told us, and there's a more traditional ballad on that same cassette too, about two lovers who die young and tragically and are buried next to each other in the same graveyard, that's the song playing right now in the car in the July dark as we drive back to the caravan site, the man from The Spinners singing the words *and from her heart grew a red red rose. And from his heart grew a briar. They grew and they grew on the old church wall. Till they could grow no higher.* When we get back to the caravan and get into our beds in the smell of toothpaste and soap-bags, when the breathing of all the others regulates and becomes rhythmic, I will be wide awake thinking about the dead lovers, they are wearing football strips, bright red, and their hearts are a tangle of briars and thorns, and one of my brothers shifts in his sleep and turns to me in the makeshift bed and says from somewhere near sleep, are you having a bad dream? and then though I don't say anything at all he takes me and turns me round, puts one arm under me so my head is on his shoulder and his other arm across my front, and that's how he holds me, sleeping himself, until I fall asleep too.

Every flower open on me nods its heavy head.

I lie in my bed in a home I'm learning to let go of and I listen to my neighbour playing the drums through the wall in the middle of the night. He's not bad. He's getting better, getting the hang of it.

Every rose opens into a layering of itself, a dense-packed grandeur that holds until it spills. On days that are still I can trace, if I want, exactly where I've been just by doubling back on myself and following the trail I've left.

But I prefer the windy days, the days that strip me back, blasted, tossed, who knows where, imagine them, purple-red, silver-pink, natural confetti, thin, fragile, easily crushed and blackened, fading already wherever the air's taken them across the city, the car parks, the streets, the ragged grass verges, dog-ear and adrift on the surfaces of the puddles, flat to the gutter stones, mixing with the litter, their shards of colour circling in the leaf-grimy corners of yards.

York City Children's Library made me the writer I am, Kate Atkinson told me. Then she told me about the adult ticket they decided they'd issue her there at the age of six because she was taking out so many books.

She went on to describe how the quite small area in that City Library which was originally the children's section is the place where all the library's books are now, that everywhere else is filled with computers or space dedicated to genealogy, and how it's not called the City Library any more, how now it's called the York Experience.

Her daughter Helen Clyne interrupted to say that the important thing about the notion of a public library now is that it's the one place you can just turn up to, a free space, a democratic space where anyone can go and be there with other people, and you don't need money –

a clean, well-lighted place, Kate said –

whose underlying municipal truth is that it isn't a shop, Helen said. And you can just go. It's somewhere you can just be. People of all ages all round you. It doesn't have to be educational. It doesn't matter who you are or what you're doing. Young or old. Rich or homeless. It doesn't matter. You can just go there.

So it's not about books any more? I said. Or it's about more than books?

It maybe always was, Helen said.

In that books have always been about people? I said.

Well, of course. But there was a culture that encouraged us, and now it doesn't exist, Kate said. I bought very few books when the girls were young. We went to the library. And nobody bought books when I was young either. I went to the library.

It was what we did, Helen said. It was a habit, a ritual. You borrowed it, you read it, you brought it back and chose something else, and someone else read whatever you read after and before you. It was communal. That's what public library means: something communal.

The poet

So she'd taken the book and she'd thrown it across the room and when it hit the wall then fell to the floor with its pages open it nearly broke, which was one of the worst things you could do, maybe a worse thing even than saying a blasphemous curse, no, than saying a blasphemous curse in a church, or near a church, to break a book.

And she was a strong lass and she had a good throw on her, as good a throw as a boy any day, easily as good as thon holiday boy she'd shoved into the river. For he might be at school down south but that didn't mean no folk knew Latin north of Edinburgh, did it, they had the Latin up here as well, not that he even knew what he claimed to anyway. *Aut insanit homo, aut versus facit* she'd said and he'd looked at her blank-like, the so-called boy scholar who'd never heard of Horace, who said *pater* and *mater* to rhyme with allig*ator*, with the *mater* and the *pater vacat*ioning in *Nairn*shire, so *taken* with the *area*, and then he'd said the thing about highland girls and looked at her to let her know he'd a liking, the cheek of it. For he might have a father a famous surgeon but that meant nothing when you'd no need of a surgeon, aye, and no need of a father either, or a mother. And were all Edinburgh boys that feart to hang off the parapet of a bridge by their arms? He was too feart even to try, him and his sister afraid to climb even a tree, and a girl afraid of a tree was one thing, but a boy? *Oh no, his clothes* he said and his sister with her painted face and her talk of *boyfriends*, standing doing a dance, *everybody's doing it back at home, don't you know it, Olive, really truly don't you up here och dear me that's too too*, then she started doing it, a mad thing with her shoulders and her legs, right there in the long grass at the river, the midges jazzing up and down in a cloud above the sister's head, and then the brother joined in, he knew the steps too, he shimmied up the riverbank away from the sister, took her own arm as if to make her do it too and then – Well, then he'd found himself in the river, and his good clothes too.

Then she'd run for home, blasphem-o blasphem-as blasphem-at, over and over under her breath to the sound of her own feet hitting the path past the ruined church, blasphem-amus, blasphem-atus, blasphem-ant, it wasn't grammatical or real Latin like but it made a fine sound. She was laughing some, though she was shocked a bit at herself for doing it, in her head she could see the shock on the face of the boy from the cold of the water when he scrambled to his feet on the slippy stones, the water had darkened his good trews and his jacket too all up the side of himself he'd fallen on.

But it was when she was blasphemating up the High Street she saw the father of the man who was her father. He had his back to her, he was looking in the windows of the butcher's. And when she got back to the house her Aunt was out and her mother she could hear shifting about upstairs like a piece of misery as usual, and something, a badness, had come over her right then and she'd hated them all (except her Aunt, she'd never hate her Aunt) and she'd gone to the shelf where the books were kept and she'd taken the first one off the shelf her hand had come to and she'd thrown it.

And the book had broken right open and that's when she'd seen there was a music inside it, one nobody knew about, one you could never have guessed at, that was part of the way that the book had been made.

They were Fraser books. They'd sent them, the Frasers. There were books, and good new clothes too came to the house sometimes, and one day last month – it wasn't a birthday, it was well past her birthday, but Aunt said it would be meant for her sixteenth – there was even a watch, Aunt said a real gold one and put it away upstairs in its velvet in its hard box still in the shop wrapping from Aberdeen, for they knew otherwise it'd end in the river or buried in sand on the beach, sand choking its dainty face and nobody finding it for who knows how many summers or winters, if ever.

St Agnes Eve! Ah, bitter chill it was. The owl, for all his feathers, was a-cold. The hare limp'd trembling through the frozen grass. That was the poem Keats had written, about her birthdate, 20 January, four long months ago her birthday, and one thing certain, time meant something more than the face of a wee gold watch, aye they could send a watch fine, even one that'd obviously cost a fair bit, but if they saw her in the street they'd look right through her, her father too. Since she was a quite wee girl he'd been back and as close as Flemington right up the road, so close a bird would hardly notice it, hardly have to use its wings if it crossed the sky from here to there.

But he may as well still be in Australia with the sheep for all the difference his coming back made to his daughter, in fact she wished he were, so there'd be no danger of seeing him, no chance of him and his not-seeing her, in a street so close to home. She wished him thousands of miles away from here, truthfully she wished him on Algol, the bad most evil star in the sky, and her mother too, they could go and live there just the two of them and happily never exchange a word to each other for as long as they lived and nobody else would have to care. They could just go, the both, and take all their unsaying with them. For if a flower grew near them, even just the air that came from them would wither that flower.

But did that mean she would wither things too?

Did a badness pass from them to her?

Would it ruin the feel of the mouth of the hill pony on the palm of her hand when she went the hike by herself and gave it the apple she had for her lunch, the bluntness of the mouth, the breath of it, the whiskers round the mouth she could feel, the warm wet and the slaver on her hand that she wiped on her skirt and got into the trouble about?

And the nest shaped like a dome, something that the bird just made without needing to know, without reading in a book how to make, and made it so solid and hung it so firm in the thinnest of the branches over the river?

There was the word gorgeous, and there was the word north, and there was a sound that went between the words that she liked. Could you wither a word?

There was the orchard nobody went to. How could anything touch it? It was all blossom right now. There was the whole meadow full of flowers, wild ones, all the bright faces, out that window beyond this house only a couple of streets away. She sat low on the old nursing chair and the Fraser books sat on the shelf right next to her eye. Fraser. Olive. O LIVE. I LOVE. O VILE. EVIL O.

She reached and took out the first book. She didn't even look at it, she threw the book. She just threw it.

And that's how, when the spine fell off it and she picked it up to look at the bad damage she'd done, she saw – music.

Inside, behind the spine, the place where the pages were bound was lined with it, notes and staves all the way down the place where the name of the book had been. There'd been a music inside it all the years the book had been in the world. And that was a fair few years, for on one of its first pages was the date 1871. So that made it fifty-four years, near sixty, there'd been music nobody'd known about in the back of – she looked at the broken piece of spine – Walter Scott's Ivanhoe. And the paper with the notes on it looked like it might be a good bit older than the book whose spine it was hidden in, for there was a quality to the way the staves and notes were formed that didn't look like these things looked nowadays.

That was an e, but she didn't have the beginning of the stave so she didn't know what key. C#, f, e, c#, b, b, f#, a. Then the piece of music ended where the paper had been cut to fit the spine. On the surviving bit of stave below: a, a, e, g, b, e, b.

She went to the space on the shelf that Ivanhoe had left empty. She put her finger to the top of the spine of the book next to the space, tipped the book out, watched it balance on its own weight then fall. She caught it in her hand. Waverley Novels. The Heart of Mid-Lothian. She ran her hand over the good spine. The paper of it felt like brushed leather. Maybe it was leather. It looked expensive. It looked like it would never break.

You could not tell whether there was music inside it just by looking at it.

The clean closed spines all along the Scott collection, book after book, quiet and waiting, lined three shelves. She shouldn't even be in the front room. It was kept for the good. It wasn't used.

(The boy's face, surprised by the cold of the water. The dipper's nest overhanging the river, disguised by leaves in summer, bare to the eye in winter. The carcasses hanging in the butcher's window with the red and the white where the meat met the fat. The workings of the watch in its box in the dark.)

She looked at how well the stitching of the binding met the spine on the book in her hand. She gave it a tug with her fingers.

She went to the kitchen to get the gutting knife.

*

Olive Fraser, born 20 January 1909, Aberdeen. Died 9 December 1977, Aberdeen.

Brought up by her beloved aunt, Ann Maria Jeans, in Redburn, Queen Street, Nairn, on the Moray Firth coast in the Scottish Highlands. Estranged parents leave her there when they emigrate (separately) to Australia, and continue to do so after they come back (still estranged).

A force of energy and adventure, a headlong kind of a girl. *That lassie lives in figures of speech.* Blue-eyed blonde, so eye-catching that the newly instated Rector of the University of Aberdeen (which is where she goes in 1927 when she's finished school, to study English), who happens to be driving past in his carriage from his own Instatement Ceremony, turns his head and cranes his neck to catch another glimpse of such a startlingly beautiful girl in the crowd.

A talker. A livewire. *She was a beauty, but she gave the men a run for it.* Hilariously funny. A poet. Circle of admiring undergraduates at her feet and her lines spilling out of her all Spenserian stanza. Annoying to young men in seminars: *she niver thocht that up hersel, far did she get it fae?* Beloved of landladies (and simultaneously disapproved of): *that Miss Fraser! she keepit awfa 'ours.* Bright, glowing like a lightbulb, ideas flickering like power surges. When trying to string fishing line on a rod and reel in her student lodgings, tangles herself up so badly that she has to toss a coin out of a window to a passing boy to get him to send a telegram to her friend Helena, a couple of years younger and a writer herself, enthralled by her exciting older poet friend: *imprisoned in digs. Please rescue. Olive.* Recalls, much later in life, this friend's happy family house in Aberdeen, the welcoming shouts and the laughter, the merriness, the warmth. Recalls her friend's mother's singing, and the lucky stone with a hole in it that her friend's mother gives her before her final exams.

Outstanding student. 1933: to Girton College in Cambridge on scholarship money, though a couple of years remain unaccounted for in between Aberdeen and Cambridge – poor health? poverty? mental exhaustion? Intermittently ill. Pale. Fatigued for no reason.

Five days of psychoanalysis in London: *he simply took my mind to pieces and built it up again. I really feel as if I had been presented with a new heaven and a new earth, ten thousand cold showers on spring mornings and a Tinglow friction brush (mental).*

Gains reputation as talented young poet. Wins Chancellor's Medal for English Verse in 1935, only the second female student ever. Poem is called The Vikings. Senate unused to presenting anything to women: *a kind of quasi academic dress had to be devised*. Takes to calling herself Olave. Makes many new friends. Gets on many new people's nerves: *she was a pain in the neck*. Strongly dislikes Cambridgeshire, too flat, too dank, too inland. Strongly dislikes Girton (remembers it ten years later, in a poem called On a Distant Prospect of Girton College, like this: Here does heavenly Plato snore, / A cypher, no more. / . . . / Here sits Dante in the dim / With Freud watching him. / . . . / Here does blessed Mozart seem / Alas, a sensual dream.). Girton, in turn, strongly dislikes her: *she wasted the time of promising young scholars*.

Bad headaches. Grey skin. Nosebleeds. Concentration lapses. Unexplained illness. Fatigue.

Drifts from job to job. Back north to help on farm. Trains polo-ponies in Oxfordshire. Assistant to archaeologist in Bedford. Wartime: applies to cypher dept in Royal Navy WRNS in Greenwich. Posted to Liverpool, junior officer on watch, witnesses blitzing of maternity hospital near Liverpool docks. *Went out of her mind . . . thought the enemy were after her, trying to get in touch with her*. 1945: Poultry worker. 1946: Bodleian librarian (gets the sack, leaves under a cloud). Solderer. Assistant nurse. Cleric. Shop girl (Fortnum's, among others). 1949: living in Stockwell Street, Greenwich (now demolished), then Royal Hill, Greenwich. *Made most of the furniture myself, being employed by a firm that had its own sawmill and was very generous in a thoughtful kind way to its employees and even to people who lived around.* The death of the mother. The death of her aunt. The death of her dog, Quip, an Irish terrier. Drawn to Roman Catholicism; poetry becomes devotional. Poverty. *One new outfit in the last twelve years.*

1956 in London: onset of severe mental illness. *I was walking along and I just blacked out and when I came to, I found myself up a tree.* Diagnosed with schizophrenia. Hospitalized. *I cannot write any literature. It is as though I had lost a limb.* Medication: chlorpromazine. Like she's been *hammered down in a box and dropped below the Bermuda Deep.* Unrecognizable, *changed from the gallant, yellow-haired, rosy-cheeked girl. Grossly overweight, disfigured.* Medication brings on painful sensitivity to sunlight. Puffy eyes. Skin grey, leathery. Stuffs enough hospital teddy bears (paltry sum per bear) nearly to ruin her hands. Buys herself ticket north.

1960s: moves from house to uneasy house, renting in Inverness, Capital of the Highlands, sixteen miles from Nairn. Hospitalized again. Seen in grounds of Craig Dunain, Inverness mental hospital, wandering about holding beaten-up typewriter. Moves back to Aberdeen, this time to Cornhill Hospital. *Percipient woman doctor* thinks schizophrenia might be misdiagnosis and medicates for hypothyroidism, myxoedema. *As if by disenchantment* herself again.

Sunlight. *Three wonderful years of good health.*

Cancer. Two operations. Dies in December 1977. Penniless at time of death. Friends gather in snow for funeral that never takes place: bad weather, mishap, misinformation, accident.

Winner, over the years, of twenty-two literary prizes and two gold medals. Very little work published. *When I send a poem to a publisher with 'Royal Mental Hospital' at the top . . .*

I have forgotten how to be / A bird upon a dawn-lit tree, / A happy bird that has no care / Beyond the leaf, the golden air. / I have forgotten moon and sun, / And songs concluded and undone, / And hope and ruth and all things save / The broken wit, the waiting grave.

*

In her gold medal-winning early poem, The Vikings, the dead are simultaneously ancient and young, *younger than death and life.* The poem's narrator asks them how it's possible that they're so very beautiful:

> O we are loved among the living still,
> We are forgiven among the dead. We plough
> In the old narrows of the spirit. We
> Have woven our wealth into your mystery.

Here are three of her poems, the first from 1943, the second circa 1954, the third 1971.

THE PILGRIM

I have no heart to give thee, for I
Am only groundmists and a thing of wind,
And the stone echoes under bridges and the kind
Lights of high farms, the weary watchdog's cry.

I have no desire for thy dreams, for my own
Are no dreams, but realities which are
The blind man's sight, the sick man's heavenly star
Fire of the homeless, to no other known.

THE POET (III)

Go to bed, my soul,
When the light is done.
Sleep from enemies
Blanketed in bone.

Let thy blood grow cold
As a mouldering stone
On a martyr's tomb,
Known to God alone.

On the stair of truth
Down and up are one.
Bless the cobbled street
When the light is gone.

When the light is past
When the flower is shown
Let the poet be
Common earth and stone.

THE UNWANTED CHILD

I was the wrong music
The wrong guest for you
When I came through the tundras
And thro' the dew.

Summon'd, tho' unwanted,
Hated, tho' true
I came by golden mountains
To dwell with you.

I took strange Algol with me
And Betelgeuse, but you
Wanted a purse of gold
And interest to accrue.

You could have had them all,
The dust, the glories too,
But I was the wrong music
And why I never knew.

*

The story about her finding the music in the spines of the books is made up by me.

But that 1871 edition of Scott, like many books over the centuries, bound with recycled old paper stock, really is lined and pasted with staved manuscript at the back of the pages, at least, the ones I've got on my desk are. And she really could, as a girl, hang from the parapet of a Nairn bridge by her arms, and pretty much everything else here can be found and is sourced in the collections of her poems which her good friend from her university years in Aberdeen and Cambridge, the Medieval and Renaissance academic Helena Mennie Shire, edited after Olive Fraser's death, The Pure Account (Aberdeen University Press, 1981) and The Wrong Music (Canongate, 1989).

Think of the Waverley collection on the shelves, the full twenty-five novels, their spines sliced back and open and the music inside them visible.

In a poem pamphlet by Sophie Mayer called TV GIRLS, full of poems about contemporary TV heroines, Mayer lists the weapons that Buffy the Vampire Slayer uses throughout the show's seven TV seasons to keep the vampires, demons and various forces of evil at bay. On her list, in among the stakes and swords and sunlight, is 'library card'.

I wrote and asked her about the library card as weapon. This is what she replied:

> *Libraries save the world, a lot, but outside the narrative mode of heroism: through contemplative action, anonymously and collectively. For me, the public library is the ideal model of society, the best possible shared space, a community of consent – an anarcho-syndicalist collective where each*

person is pursuing their own aim (education, entertainment, affect, rest) with respect to others, through the best possible medium of the transmission of ideas, feelings and knowledge: the book.

I believe that within every library is a door that opens to every other library in time and space: that door is the book. The library is what Michel Foucault called a 'heterotopia', an ideal yet real and historically delimited place that allows us to step into ritual time (like the cinema and the garden). It is a site of possibility and connection (and possibility in connection).

Without public libraries, I would not have known there was a world outside the conservative religious community in which I grew up (and of which I would probably still be a part without the heroic librarians in our small suburban library who faced out work by Jane Rule and Melanie Kaye/Kantrowitz and Leslie Feinberg even after the passage of Section 28). I believe libraries are essential for informed and participatory democracy, and that there is therefore an ideological war on them via cuts and closures, depriving individuals and communities of their right to knowledge and becoming on their own terms.

The human claim

I had been planning to write this story about the ashes of DH Lawrence. I hadn't known what had happened to him after he was dead. Now that I did – at least, if what the biography I'd been reading claimed was true – I couldn't get it out of my head. On the train home that night, even though it was a couple of months since I'd finished reading it, I'd got my notebook out of my bag and made some notes about it and about some other things too that the biography said had happened to him.

For instance, he'd be walking past a theatre or picturehouse in London in the First World War and the crowd would jeer at his beard, which marked him out, made him a visible slacker, a refuser, not enlisted, maybe even a conscientious objector. Then, the cottage he'd taken for some of the war years had been raided by the Home Office or the military authorities who'd confiscated not just some letters in German (his wife, Frieda, was related to the German military) but also a copy of a Hebridean song, because they thought it was secret code, and some drawings Lawrence had made of the stems of plants which, the biographer said, they'd decided were secret maps.

I'd thought I knew quite a lot about Lawrence's actual life. I've been reading him since I was sixteen, when I chose a dual copy of St Mawr / The Virgin and the Gypsy for a school prize, mostly because I knew it would discomfit the Provost and his wife, who annually gave out the prizes; Lawrence was still reasonably notorious in Inverness in the 1970s. (It makes me laugh even now that the prize sticker inside my paperback says I'm being awarded for Oral French.) Now I was six years older than he'd been when he died. I'd felt for him all through reading this fine and thoughtful biography. Sitting on the train weeks later I was still preoccupied with him, his little red beard jutting in fury at all the patriotic clichés. All these weeks later it still made me laugh with real satisfaction that the authorities had been stupid enough to think Gaelic was some kind of secret code.

Above all, though, it was the story of what may have happened to his body five years after his death that I couldn't stop thinking about. I was still amazed by it now, cycling my bike home from the station.

But then I got home and opened my mail and I stopped thinking about anything because there was a Barclaycard statement waiting for me which claimed I'd spent a fortune.

I only very rarely use that credit card, or any of my credit cards. I'm quite good credit-wise, honest. In fact, that card had actually been a hundred pounds *in* credit for months, which is why I'd recently used it to buy some shirts for Christmas in a clothes shop in London called Folk.

I looked at the total again. £1,597.67. Had I really spent that much money on four shirts?

I turned the statement over. **Previous balance from last statement** £100.37. 11 Dec Folk, London £531.00. 21 Dec Lufthansa, Koeln £1,167.04 1,840.70 U. S. Dollar, USA, Exch Rate 0.6340 Incl Non Sterling Trans Fee of £33.88 **03 Jan New Balance £1,597.67.**

Lufthansa.

I hadn't bought anything from Lufthansa ever.

I phoned the Barclaycard number at the top of my statement.

Hi there!

An automaton instructed me that I could answer its questions either by pressing the buttons on my phone or by speaking into the gaps it would leave for me. It had been recorded by someone with a north-of-England voice, friendly, like a not too abrasive stand-up comedian. I gave this matey automaton my card number and it offered me some options. When none of these involved speaking to someone about a fraudulent claim and I didn't answer quickly enough either with button pushing or by saying something, the automaton asked me to tell it out loud what I wanted.

I'd like to speak to someone, I said.

I'm sorry, I didn't quite catch that, the automaton said. Try again.

I'd like to speak to someone, I said again.

I'm sorry, I didn't quite catch that, the northern automaton said. Try again. Try saying something like: *Pay my bill.*

Speak to someone, I said.

I'm sorry, I didn't quite catch that, the automaton said.

I stayed silent.

I'm sorry, I didn't quite catch that, the automaton said. Hold on. I'll just put you through to a member of our team who'll be able to help you. Just so you know, all our calls are recorded for training and legal purposes.

I listened to the muzak for a bit.

Hello, you're speaking to indecipherable, how can I help you? a real person said to me down the phone from somewhere that had the sound of very far away.

He asked me some security questions, to check it was really me.

There's a transaction on here, I said, that I didn't make and I didn't authorize.

Don't worry, Ms Smith, he said. Thank you, Ms Smith. I can see that, Ms Smith. Yes, Ms Smith, thank you.

He put me through to some more muzak. Some minutes later a woman answered. She also had the slight delay round her voice which signalled that although she was here in my ear, I was maybe on the phone to somebody on a totally different planet. She asked me the same security questions. Then she told me that this card had been presented for use yesterday for a transaction costing two pounds –

Two pounds! I said and this is what went through my head as I said it: *I'd never use a credit card for something so small.* It was as if *I* needed proof that I hadn't used my credit card even though I knew full well that I hadn't.

Meanwhile, the woman was still speaking.

– card was then withdrawn just before the transaction went through, she said.

It wasn't me, I said. I'd just like to make that really clear.

She told me Barclaycard would be in touch with me, that I'd hear from them over the next three weeks and that I was to be sure to reply within the requested timeframe or they would consider the matter resolved and charge my card accordingly.

For a transaction that I didn't make? I said.

Be sure to reply within the requested timeframe, Ms Smith, she said.

And look – it's in dollars, I said. I haven't been to the States since 2002. I want it noted right now that I made no such transaction and that my card has been defrauded. I want this sum of money, for a ticket I never bought and a transaction I never carried out, wiped off my account. And I want you to stop this card this instant.

Yes, I can do that, Ms Smith, the woman said. There. Just a moment. Now. The card is now stopped. Please now destroy this card, Ms Smith. Barclaycard will send you a new card within the next five days or so.

I don't want a new card, I said. Someone'll probably just get its details and defraud it too. And how did Lufthansa get my details? Why did Lufthansa believe that this was me buying a ticket when it wasn't?

It will now go forward for further investigation so that we can ascertain the facts of this situation, thank you, Ms Smith, the woman said.

It wasn't me, I said again.

I sounded petulant. I sounded like a child.

Thank you for being in touch with Barclaycard, Ms Smith, she said. Have a lovely evening.

I pressed the hang-up button on my phone and found I was in my front room.

What I mean is, even though I'd been there the whole time, I'd actually just spent the last half hour somewhere which made my own front room irrelevant, even to me.

I stood by the fireplace and it was as if I had been filled with live ants. I went antsily around the house from room to room for about half an hour. Then I stopped, stood by the dark window, sat down on the edge of the couch. I told myself there was nothing to do about it but laugh it off. It happens all the time. People are always getting scammed. That's life.

I picked up a book but I couldn't concentrate to read.

I began to wonder instead who the person was, the person who'd pretended, somewhere else in the world, to be me. What did he or she look like? Was he or she part of a group of people who did this kind of thing? Or was it a single individual somewhere in a room by him- or herself? Somewhere in the world this person knew enough about the numbers on a card in my wallet in the dark of my pocket to fool a respectable airline company into selling an expensive ticket.

I looked at the statement again. It didn't say anything about where the ticket was from or to. Dec 21. Maybe this other me had been going home for Christmas. Did she have a family? Did the family know she was a fraudster? Were they maybe a family of fraudsters? I could see them all round a long table set for Christmas; I stood ghost at their feast and watched them with their arms round their shoulders as Hogmanay gave way to New Year. How could she be me? I hadn't sat in Departures with a print-out ticket paid for by me. I hadn't walked down the tunnel that led to the door of the aeroplane, or climbed the steps out in the cold of the winter airport air.

Oh Christ. Passport.

I ran upstairs. I pulled open the cupboard door. But my passport was safe there on the underwear shelf.

I put it back. I closed the door. I laughed. Oh well. I came downstairs and put the kettle on, thought about making something to eat. But it was after nine o'clock and if I ate now I'd not sleep.

So I sat on the kitchen stool until the kettle boiled and I thought about how once, years ago, I had been really well pickpocketed in an Italian seaside resort by a child. The child, a dark-haired girl with a miniature accordion slung on her shoulder, had been walking up and down outside the restaurant we'd decided to eat at, playing the opening riff of Volare. I must've looked an easy touch; she had approached me and asked for money and when I'd said no she had talked to me briefly and shyly while thieving from me with such sleight of hand that it wasn't till I'd put my hand in my pocket half an hour later for the roll of cash I was carrying so I could pay the bill and found the pocket empty that I knew. She'd done it with such artistry that I almost didn't regret what she'd taken. On the contrary, I'd felt strangely blessed. It was as if I'd been specially chosen.

How was this different? It felt different. It felt like it had been nothing to do with me. There'd been no real exchange. More, it somehow made *me* the suspect. No amount of speaking down a phone to someone in a call centre could restore my innocence.

I got my Barclaycard out of my wallet and folded it in two. I folded it back on itself the other way. I did this several times very fast until the fold gave off heat. When I could no longer put the tip of my finger on it because it was so hot, I ripped the card in two, one half *valid from*, the other *expires end*.

Five days later a new card with a new number and my name on it arrived from Barclaycard.

Ten days after that, a form arrived. It asked me to tick a box which confirmed whether I agreed or disagreed that I had made the transaction in question with Lufthansa.

I ticked the box which disagreed. I wrote underneath in capitals: I HAVE NEVER IN MY LIFE CARRIED OUT ANY TRANSACTION

WITH LUFTHANSA WITH THIS OR ANY OTHER CARD and I signed the form with my name.

Two weeks after that, a letter arrived from Barclaycard which said they'd *credited my Barclaycard with the amount involved* while they made *further enquiries*.

Meanwhile, here's the story of what maybe happened to the remains of DH Lawrence.

After he died in 1930 at the age of forty-four, his wife, Frieda, married her lover, Angelo Ravagli, and they moved to New Mexico. In 1935 she sent her husband back to Vence in France, where Lawrence had died and was buried, with the instruction that he have Lawrence's body exhumed and cremated so that she could put his ashes in a beautiful vase.

Ravagli took the vase to Vence. He came back to New Mexico with the vase full of ashes. Frieda sealed the ashes up in a resplendent memorial shrine inside a block of concrete in case of thieves. When she died in 1956 she was buried next to this shrine. There's a photograph of the shrine on Wikipedia. It has a risen phoenix carved in stone or concrete above it and the letters DHL surrounded by bright painted sunflowers and foliage on the front.

But in the biography I'd been reading, which is by John Worthen, Worthen says that after Frieda died, Ravagli announced: 'I threw away the DH cinders.' He'd had him exhumed and burned as instructed, he claimed, but then he'd dumped the ashes – maybe in Marseilles, Worthen thinks, maybe at the harbour, into the sea. When he got back to New York, Ravagli filled the vase with the ashes of God knows what or who. He gave it to Frieda, who buried it with honours and died believing she'd be being buried next to what was left of Lawrence.

Wikipedia, too, seems to suggest that the ashes in that shrine are actually Lawrence's.

Who knows? Maybe they are.

But whether they are or they aren't, imagine the husband, faithful and lying, seething, triumphant, steady in deception for twenty whole years till she dies. Imagine his foul understandable need, his satisfaction, changing DH Lawrence to DH cinders.

Imagine the ashes of Lawrence shaken into the air, dissolving in the ocean.

'Fish, oh Fish, / So little matters!'

That's from the poem called Fish. In another poem he calls the mosquito he's hunting 'Monsieur', then 'Winged Victory'. 'Am I not mosquito enough to out-mosquito you?' In another he declares that for his part he prefers his heart to be broken, cracked open like a pomegranate spilling its red seeds. In one of his most famous, he watches a snake drink at a waterhole then throws a log at it to show it who's boss. The moment he does this he understands his own pettiness; he knows he's cheated himself.

Sexual intercourse began in 1963 because of him. Literary merit went to court and won because of him. Class in the English novel radically shifted because of him. His mother, poor, ruined by work, dirt and poverty, could be delighted by a tuppenny bunch of spring flowers; at least that's what Frieda says in an article she wrote in 1955 for the New Statesman, where she's responding to a newly published 1950s biography of Lawrence which, according to her, is full of laughable untruths and inaccuracies. 'There is nothing to save, now all is lost, / but a tiny core of stillness in the heart / like the eye of a violet.' That's from a poem called Nothing to Save. 'High in the sky a star seemed to be walking. It was an aeroplane with a light. Its buzz rattled above. Not a space, not a speck of this country that wasn't humanized, occupied by the human claim. Not even the sky.' That's from St Mawr, a novel about how human beings will never be able to be fully natural or free while they give in to civilization's pressures and expectations, also about how women and stallions will never understand each other, especially when the woman is handicapped by being clever.

His clever friend Katherine Mansfield suggested to him that he call the cottage he was living in The Phallus. Her letters and notebooks are full of her anger and frustration at him. At the same time she typically writes this kind of thing in her letters to friends. 'He is the only writer living whom I really profoundly care for. It seems to me whatever he writes, no matter how much one may "disagree" is important. And after all even what one objects to is a *sign of life* in him.' And: 'what makes Lawrence a *real* writer is his passion. Without passion one writes in the air or on the sands of the seashore.'

He himself wrote this in a letter in 1927 to Gertie Cooper, a friend and neighbour from his home in the north of England who was about to start treatment for tuberculosis, from which he also suffered and which killed him in the end: 'while we live we must be game. And when we come to die, we'll die game too.' There's a fury, a burning energy associated with TB suffering. Some see it as one of the driving forces of Lawrence's temperament and his writing. The same could be said for a writer like Mansfield, who also died far too young of the same condition, a condition completely curable so few years later.

Meanwhile, a little less than a hundred years later, I was sitting at my desk on the one hand pondering hopeless fury and in the other literally holding my latest letter from Barclaycard.

According to Barclaycard, Lufthansa claimed that I *had* reserved a ticket with them and that they had issued me this ticket, as yet unused, on 21 December last year. So, did I agree with the merchant (Lufthansa) that I had bought this ticket? If I didn't, I was to write back and tell Barclaycard and I was to do this within ten days of the date at the top of this letter.

The letter had taken eight days to arrive. I had two days left to reply and one of them was a Sunday.

Phish, oh phish. So little matters! Was there even any connection here, between the life, death and dissemination of Lawrence and me battling a fraudulent claim on a credit card statement? All I knew was, it cheered me up to think of Lawrence, whose individualism meant he'd fight anyone with both hands tied behind his back and whose magnetic pull always towards some kind of sympathy meant he'd grant a mosquito formal address in French and even compare it to an ancient work of art in the Louvre before he swatted it.

Imagine Lawrence in the virtual world. The very thought of him railing at an internet porn site, yelling at the net and all its computer games for not being nearly gamey enough, meant I forgot for a moment the letter in my hand from Barclaycard.

But back to Google Earth. I googled the address for the Lufthansa Office in London. I was thinking I could maybe go in, in person, and explain to them personally that it hadn't been me who'd bought or reserved any ticket with them, used or unused, on 21 December or ever. Google told me that the London office is in Bath Road, at the postcode UB7 0DQ. I looked it up on Google Maps. It's near Heathrow; Google Street View indicates it's a huge warehouse or hangar at the back of the airport, off the kinds of street that are practically motorway, the kinds almost nobody walks along.

The photos on Google Street View had been taken in the early summer; the trees were leafy and the may was in bloom on the low dual carriageway bushes outside the Holiday Inn. At one point you could see right inside people's cars. Google Street View had protected privacy by pixellating the numberplates of the cars. But at one point two cars were level at a junction and a man was in one, a woman in the other, and a lone pedestrian was waiting behind them at a bus stop. It was good to see some people coinciding, even unknowingly, just going somewhere one day, caught by a surveillance car and immortalized online (well, until Google Street View updated itself). Seeing them made me wonder briefly what was happening in their lives on the day this picture was taken. I wondered what had happened to them since. I hoped they'd been okay in the recession. I hoped they'd arrived safely wherever they were going.

Then I wondered if any of them was going to Lufthansa to complain about being charged for a ticket he or she hadn't bought.

Of course in the end I wasn't going to go there and explain anything. Of course it would make no difference. Of course it was impossible anyway to see anything of Lufthansa's London Office on Google

Street View since it was on a bit of the map to which the little virtual person couldn't be dragged.

So instead I skimmed along Bath Road for a bit, first one way, then the other, until at one point the address label at the top of the photograph told me that though I was still on Bath Road I was no longer in West Drayton and that I was now in Harmondsworth.

Harmondsworth. Something inside me chimed a kind of harmony. It took me a moment, then I remembered why: Harmondsworth is the place all the old Penguin paperbacks declare their place of issue. It was where the original Penguin copies of, for instance, Lady Chatterley's Lover, which caused all the excitement and led to the obscenity trial, will have issued from in 1960, the place where the thousands of copies sold after the trial will have been issued too. And all the other Penguin Lawrences. I looked across at where L was, on my shelves. Almost all my Lawrence books were Penguin books. Pretty much all the Lawrence I'd ever read had come, one way or another, from this very place I happened to be looking at.

I stood up, pushed back my chair. I got my old copy of St Mawr / The Virgin and the Gypsy off the shelf. Oral French. I turned the page. Harmondsworth.

It was a ridiculous, glorious connection, and one that somehow made me bigger and truer than any false claim being made against me. It also made me laugh. I laughed out loud. I did a little dance round the room.

When I'd stopped, I closed the book and put it back in its place on the shelf. I stood at my desk for a moment. I reread the letter. I girded my loins. I sat down to reply.

Dear Barclaycard,

This is just to thank you and Lufthansa for the reminder that nothing in life is ever secure.

Thank you also for allowing me to find out how easy it is to be made to seem like a liar when you aren't one.

Thank you, too, for introducing me to a whole new kind of anxiety, a burning and impotent fury which I truly believe has helped me understand, just for a moment, a sliver of what it must have felt like for a couple of writers I like very much from the first half of the twentieth century to have suffered from consumption. The experience has certainly brought a new layering of meaning to the word consumer for me.

Yours faithfully,
A. Smith.
PS. If Lufthansa ever tell you where that ticket I didn't buy was for, just out of natural curiosity, I'd love to know.

It felt good when I wrote it.

When I read it half an hour later I knew it was too anal, like an awful comedy letter someone would send in to a consumer rights programme on Radio 4.

I deleted it.

I wrote the kind of letter I was supposed to write, in which I simply denied knowledge of the transaction Lufthansa claimed I'd made. I sealed the envelope and I put it on the hall table for recorded delivery tomorrow.

Then I went to bed, put the light out, slept.

Meanwhile, in my sleep, the freed-up me's went wild.

They spraypainted the doors and windows of the banks, urinated daintily on the little mirror-cameras on the cash machines. They emptied the machines, threw the money on to the pavements. They stole the fattened horses out of the abattoir fields and galloped them down the high streets of all the small towns. They ignored traffic lights. They waved to surveillance. They broke into all the call centres. They sneaked up and down the liftshafts, slipped into the systems. They randomly wiped people's debts for fun. They replaced the automaton messages with birdsong. They whispered dissent, comfort, hilarity, love, sparkling fresh unscripted human responses into the ears of the people working for a pittance answering phones for businesses whose CEOs earned thousands of times more than their workforce. They flew inside aircraft fuselages and caused turbulence on every flight taken by everyone who ever ripped anyone else off. They replaced every music track on every fraudster's phone, iPad or iPod with Sheena Easton singing Modern Girl. They marauded into porn shoots and made the girls and women laugh. They were tough and delicate. They were winged like the seeds of sycamores. There were hundreds of them. Soon there would be thousands. They spread like mushrooms. They spread like spores. There would be no stopping them.

Meanwhile, that snake that Lawrence threw the log at disappeared long long ago into its hole unhurt, went freely about its ways, left the poem behind it.

Meanwhile, right now, the ashes of DH Lawrence could be anywhere.

Local councils, under the pressure of draconian and politically expedient cuts, don't like to say that the libraries they're closing are closing. They say they're 'divesting'. They now call what used to be public libraries 'community libraries'. This is an ameliorating way of saying volunteer-run and volunteer-funded.

Just in the few weeks that I've been ordering and re-editing these twelve stories for this book, twenty-eight libraries across the UK have come under threat of closure or passing to volunteers. Fifteen mobile libraries have also come under this same threat. That makes forty-three – in a matter of weeks.

Over the past few years, just in the time it's taken me to write these stories, library culture has suffered unimaginably. The statistics suggest that by the time this book is published there will be one thousand fewer libraries in the UK than there were at the time I began writing the first of the stories.

This is what Lesley Bryce told me when I asked her about libraries:

> *The Corstorphine public library was a holy place to me. It was an old building, hushed and dim, like a church, with high windows filtering dusty light on to the massive shelves of books below. And the library had its own rituals: the precious cards (only three each), the agony of choosing, and the stamping of dates. The librarians themselves were fearsome, yet kind, allowing the child me to take out adult books, though not without raised eyebrows. My parents were readers, but we did not have many books in the house, so the library was a gateway to a wider world, a lifeline, an essential resource, a cave of wonder. Without access to the public library as a child, my world would have been smaller, and infinitely less rich. All those riches, freely available, to everyone and anyone with a library card. All children should be so lucky.*
>
> *There's a great kids' library at the end of our street now where we live, in Notting Hill, soon to be sold, along with the adult one, though they claim to be rehousing it nearby.*

The ex-wife

At first I thought it was just that you really liked books, just that you were someone who really loved your work. I thought it was just more evidence of your passionate and sensitive nature.

At first I was quite charmed by it. It was charming. She was charming.

But here are three instances of what it was like for me.

1: I'd be deep asleep, in the place where all the healing happens, the place all the serious newspapers talk about in their health pages as crucial because that's where the things that fray or need patched in our daily lives get physically and mentally attended to and if we don't attend to them something irreparable will happen. Then something would wake me. It'd be you, suddenly sitting straight up in the bed so all the covers would be off both of us, then it'd be you not there, I mean I'd come to myself and the covers would be off me, I'd open my eyes into a blur of dark, put my hand out and feel the place going cold where you should be. Then a light would come on somewhere in the house. Then a small noise would be happening. I'd get up. I'd blur my way downstairs, one hand on the wall. I'd blur into the front room, or the kitchen, or the study. You'd be sitting at the table. There'd be a too-high pile of books on it. Even in the blur I'd be able to see that that pile was going to topple any moment. You'd be sitting beyond it, looking through a book. Your eyes would be distant, as if closed and open at the same time. I'd stand there for a bit. You'd not look up. What's going on? I'd say. It'd come out sounding blurry. Nothing, you'd say, I just need to know whether Wing was actually the original kitten of Charlie Chaplin. To know what? I'd say. In a letter to Woolf somewhere, you'd say. There's a kind of family tree, and I know Athenaeum is one of the kittens that Charlie Chaplin gave birth to. But there's another one and I'm pretty sure it's not Wing or at least not called Wing in this particular reference and I need to know what its name is and whether it's another name for Wing, or whether Wing was actually another cat altogether or maybe even another name for Charlie Chaplin. You're looking up her cats now? I'd say. Now? What the fuck time is it? I need to know, you'd say. Why exactly do you need to know this? I'd say. Because I realized I don't know it, you'd say. In what context could it possibly be useful? I'd say. I'll just be another minute, you'd say. I know pretty much where to look, it'll just take a minute. You'd pull another book out of the pile and catch the pile, shunt it back together with your elbow, wait till it was definitely not going to fall, and open the book at the index at the back. I'd go up to bed. I'd lie there unable to sleep. When you'd come up again two and a half hours later I'd be pretending not to be awake. You'd sigh back into bed and lie down next to me. Immediately you'd be asleep. But for me the windowblind would be edged with something far too bright. What would that noise be now? Birds.

2: We'd be talking about something really important, well, important to me at least. We'd be talking, for instance, about what happened to me at work, how everybody's running really scared about the cuts. I'd tell you what had happened in the office that day. And you'd say, God, you know that's exactly like in psychology. And I'd say, what in psychology, like manic depression or passive aggression? And you'd say, no, not psychology, I don't mean psychology, I mean pictures, it's exactly like in pictures, and I'd say, pictures of what? and you'd say, well, what happens is, this woman, she's a bit past it though she used to be a good singer, she got a medal for it, but now she's more middle-aged and she's trying to get a job as an extra in films so she can pay her rent, and the first thing Mansfield does is, like, the story opens and this woman is lying in bed in a rented room and she's got no rent. Oh, right, Mansfield, I'd say. Yeah, you'd say, and she wakes up and she's cold and she thinks it's maybe because she hasn't eaten properly, so then it's like a pageant of images crosses the ceiling in front of her, pictures of hot dinners sort of marching over the ceiling, and then she thinks she'd like some breakfast and then on the ceiling it's a pageant of images of big breakfasts, it's brilliant really when you consider what it's doing, it's a story about the fantasy of nourishment and what happens when that fantasy hits, like, reality, she even uses the word nourishing at one point I think. It's a fantastic critique of cinema actually. Yeah, I'd say, but I'm struggling to make the link between you telling me the plot of a short story and Johnston email-bullying me at work. Are you saying I'm a bit past it? No, you'd say, listen, if you read it you'd see, it's obvious, I'll go and get it for you. No, don't, I'd say. It's okay, really. I can sort it out for myself. I don't need to talk about it to anybody. But you'd be on your way to the shelf, and it's got this really lovely little throwaway phrase, you'd be saying, I can't remember it exactly but it kind of goes, something *fell, sepulchral*, she's so brilliant, that so-simple word fell with the word sepulchral after it, wait, it's here somewhere, I'll look it up. Look up the word sepulchral for me while you're at it, would you? I'd say. You know what sepulchral means, you'd say. Yeah, obviously, I'd say, everyone knows what sepulchral means. Well, everyone will one day, you'd say. Ha ha, yes, I'd say. Too true. And I'd have to tell myself to remember to look up what it meant later. I myself am not very interested in books, or words. When we were first together you used to tell me it was a relief, to be with me, because I wasn't.

3: There was the day I came home from work and I found you sitting holding a glossy book, and the cardboard envelope from Amazon still on the floor. The book was open on your knee, one page black, one page white. On the black page there was a picture of a twined thick piece of hair. On the white page there was another picture of a coiled palmful of hair, darker, and a black and white picture of a woman, a girl. You were crying, and it was about the most ridiculous thing I could think of, in the real world with all its awful things to really cry about. The thing is, I never imagined her in colour before, you said. The book you were holding was called Traces of a Writer. It was full of pictures of what was left of your favourite writer after she died, pictures of a brooch, a little knife, bits of fabric, a little pair of scissors, a chess set, things like that. This was the day I first called her your ex-wife. I said, it's like living with an extra person in our relationship. It's like there's always someone else. I meant it as a joke. But you were off on to the next page. You said, look, look, what's this little leather thing? It's called the fairy purse. Look. It's a purse, for a sovereign. She gave it to her friend when they were schoolgirls, her friend that stayed with her all through her life, you know. It's a bit weird, though, looking at this private stuff, isn't it? I said. You'd stopped crying. It's a bit necro, no? I said. You wiped at the sides of your eyes. It says here there's a message inside it, a note, you said. It says here it's never been taken out because it's too fragile, but that it says on it, 'Katie and Ida's fairy purse'. How do they know it says that, if they haven't ever taken it out? I said. And what if your ex-wife doesn't want people looking at her private stuff? I don't know that I'd want the general public always to be reading my letters or looking at my private writings, even if they did have research grant money to do it and they could give looking at old bits of rubbish left behind by a dead person a grandiose name like The Memory Meme And Materiology In Katherine Mansfield's Metaphorical Landscape. Stop pretending you're stupid, you said, why do you always pretend you're stupid, why do you always pretend to be less than you are, and why do you always use my passion for what I'm working on against me to duck responsibility in our relationship? Ha! I said, I do know some stuff, actually. I can read Wikipedia as well as the next person, actually, and if she's your ex-wife, then which does that make you, the vain incompetent who was always letting her down and who sold everything after she was dead and made a fortune out of it, or that poor woman she kept calling the Mountain? Because whichever one of those you are, that makes me the other, and I'm not playing that kind of weirdo role-play thank you very much. She was cruel, your ex-wife. She was a piece of work, all right. It was shortly after that that you threw the glossy book at the shelf and four of the little cups we'd bought in Mexico broke. Then I went over to the shelf, took the fifth cup, held it up above the fireplace and dropped it, and we both watched it break. It wasn't long after that particular day that you and I split up.

Not long after that, I remembered, and looked up the meaning. Something fell. Sepulchral.

*

I was walking through the park, through the bit where the fountains and the bushes are all laid out neatly. It was dusk and I was coming home from a meeting. It had been quite a tough meeting. I had had to lay off three people, most of a whole team, and we'd been told that Google Translate was basically going to be used to replace our report copywriting in all the sub-Saharan countries. I was a bit fed up. On top of this, I'd gone into the park to get a bit of space from the traffic and the people on the pavements, but I was still feeling crowded even here in the park, as if someone was walking a little too close to me. Someone *was* walking a little too close to me. There was a definite feeling of boundary-trespass in it. Then this voice, close to my ear, said: *To think one can speak with someone who really knew Tchekhov.*

I stepped to the side, turned like you do when you want to signal to people to back off.

I've no change, I said, I've no money at all to spare and there's no point in asking me.

Indecent, she said and shook her head. *We must never speak of ourselves to* anybody*: they come crashing in like cows into a garden.*

Look, I said –

How did Dostoievsky know, she interrupted me, *about that extraordinary vindictiveness, that relish for bitter laughter that comes over women in pain?*

What? I said because she had stopped me in my tracks, was standing right in front of me now blocking my way, and because it was the first time I had realized quite how in pain I was. I was actually in physical pain, walking through the park, without you.

Supposing, she said, *ones bones were not bone but liquid light.*

It was a dead person stopping me on my path, young and wiry and alarmingly lively, alarmingly bright at the eyes.

Back off, I said. I mean it. I don't know who you are, but I know who you are.

She laughed. She turned on her heel in a little dance, like I was the dead person, compared to her.

I shall be obliged, she said, *if the contents of this book are regarded as my private property.*

Then she threw me a little look.

Yes! I said. Yes exactly! Because that's what I was always saying!

I am thinking over my philosophy, she said. *The defeat of the personal. And let us be honest. How much do we know of Tchekhov from his letters. Was that all? Of course not. Don't you suppose he had a whole longing life of which there is hardly a word?*

That's what I told her, over and over! I said.

This is the moment which, after all, we live for, she said, *the moment of direct feeling when we are most ourselves and least personal.*

You've no idea, I said. I mean, one night it was even the genealogy of your cats, for God sake.

She flung her arms into the air and shouted at the sky.

Robert Louis Stevenson is a literary vagrant! she shouted.

Then she burst out laughing. I joined in.

Whatever it was she was laughing about, it was contagious.

Fiction, she said when she'd stopped laughing, *is impossible but enables us to reach what is relatively truth.*

Okay, I said, yeah, I think that's fair, I mean, if people are reading your stories and enjoying or understanding and analysing them as stories and everything. That's different. But people who were born, like, decades after you died, writing about pictures of your scissors.

I sat down on a bench. She sat down next to me with a thump and huffed a breath out loud like a teenage girl. She turned towards me nodding, confidential, like we were such friends.

What the writer does is not so much to solve *the question, but to* put *the question. There must be the question put. That seems to me a very nice dividing line between the true and the false writer.*

Then she stood up on the bench. She laughed, then got her balance. She spoke generally, to the trees in the park.

As I see it, she said, *the whole stream of English literature is trickling out in little innumerable marsh trickles. There is no gathering together, no fire, no impetus, absolutely no passion!*

She waved her arm at the bushes behind us, and her other arm at the pond in front of us.

This new bracken is like HG Wells dream

flowers, like strings of Beads, she said. *The sky in the water is like white swans in a blue mirror.*

She was right. The sky in the water *did* look like she said. The bloom on the bracken behind us *was* like beads, *did* look strange, like made up in a dream. But while I was looking at this, off she went. When I looked back there was nobody else on the bench and though the park was full of people it was like there was nobody left in it either.

*

I don't know who you are but I know who you are.

The way it was impossible haunted me.

That night I sat down in front of my computer and wrote you an email. It was the third email I'd sent you since we broke up. The first one had been fifteen pages long when I printed it out; it was mostly mundane lists of things: kitchenware, DVDs, things you'd done that'd made me furious. The second one said: Please also return the three Kate Rusby CDs, the hat that belonged to my father, the picture frame which I bought and paid the whole amount for in Habitat and have a receipt for, the TV Digibox, the food processor which I bought and paid the whole amount for in Dixons and have the receipt for, and the kitchen bin which I still can't believe you took. I will record any other items I find missing as I find them missing.

You had sent me none, not even one saying you wanted those precious books back.

This time I typed in your address (I had to do it by hand and from memory because I'd deleted you off my system) and I wrote in the subject box: not about the Kate Rusby CDs etc please read.

Then in the body of the email I wrote: Please write back telling me one single thing you think I should know about the life of the writer K Mansfield.

I pressed send, then I went to bed.

I saw the light come round the edge of the windowblind. I heard the waking of the birds.

I logged on before I left for work, and under the subject heading *one thing* you had sent me this:

Mansfield was close good friends with the writer DH Lawrence, but it was a very rocky friendship, it blew hot and cold, and there were times in their lives when neither of them could stand the other. Once, when they'd had one of their most serious fallings-out and Mansfield was full of fury at him, she was sitting in a tea room with some friends and they overheard two or three people talking about one of Lawrence's books, a collection of poems called Amores. One of them was holding it up and they were all being most disparaging about it. She herself had just been being most disparaging about Lawrence to her friends, before they went to tea. But seeing these other people be it, she leaned over and asked politely, sweetly, might she just have a look at that book they were talking about for a moment. Then she stood up and simply left the tea room, taking the book with her. The people sat there waiting for her to come back. She didn't come back.

I read this three times before I left for work. At work I read it too many times to count. I wasn't sure what it meant, but I liked it. I sat in my mid-morning break and thought about how like you it was to use the words *most disparaging*. Most disparaging. Most disparaging. *Blew hot and cold.* I sat in my lunch break. I loved the last sentence, but all the same it worried me. *She didn't come back.*

*

Wasn't it Santayana who said: every artist holds a lunatic in leash? I was back in the park with what was left of the life of your favourite writer, whose five volumes of letters and whose big thick journal I had removed from the book box by the front door when you were busy loading the van, and the space left by which I had filled with my Stieg Larsson Girl With The Dragon Tattoo books, which I knew you hated, and which I had disguised by placing all those volumes of that book Pilgrimage on top of.

I went most evenings after work now to the park, before I got the bus home. I went at lunchtimes too.

James makes me ashamed for real artists. He's a pompazoon. Who was James? I didn't care. I never knew what she was talking about, but I loved it. She was so much herself, and she was different every time, could change her air like the horse can change colour in The Wizard Of Oz. It crossed my mind to ask her, did she know what The Wizard Of Oz was. Maybe the book. She'd definitely died before the film. Strange to think she never knew Judy Garland or the tune of Somewhere Over the Rainbow, or that song about the munchkins. I wondered if anybody in your work circles had ever written a paper about that. What would it be called? Ultra-Modern Future-Memory: A Study Of Things That Happened After My Ex-Wife's Ex-Wife Died And How They Feature In The Work Of My Ex-Wife's Ex-Wife.

What makes Lawrence a real writer is his passion. Without passion one writes in the air or on the sands of the seashore. Oh, I know about you and Lawrence, I said, because a friend of mine told me a story about that. But she was off like a butterfly on to the next flowerhead. *Nathaniel Hawthorne – he is with Tolstoi the only novelist of the soul. He is concerned with what is abnormal. His people are dreams, sometimes faintly conscious that they dream.* Right, I said. I get that. Right. *The intensity of an action is its truth. Is a thing the expression of an individuality?* No, I said. Well, maybe sometimes it is. Sometimes yes and sometimes no. *Maupassant – his abundant vitality. Great artists are those who can make men see their particular illusion.* I like that, I said, looking her right in the eyes. She did have extraordinarily clear and piercing eyes. *I want to remember*, she said, *how the light fades from a room – and one fades with it.*

And one what? I said. Fades, did you say?

The sky is grey – its like living inside a pearl today, she said.

She said such beautiful things that often they left me with nothing to say. She leaned forward on the table, shook her head, held her face in her hands.

I have been feeling lately a horrible sense of indifference, she said.

Indifferent? I said. You? No way.

A very bad feeling, she said. *Neither hot nor cold; lukewarm.*

Doesn't sound at all like you, I said.

Nearly all people swing in with the tide, she said, *and out with the tide again like heavy seaweed. And they seem to take a kind of pride in denying Life.*

Yes, I said. Much better to be hot or cold, like you and your friend, what's his name. The delivery man. DHL.

Mentioning him to her was usually a good way to get her up and talking and excited. But she placed her hands on the edge of the table in fists that were little and bony.

I woke up early this morning, she said, *and when I opened the shutters the full round sun was just risen. I began to repeat that verse of Shakespeare's; lo here the gentle lark weary of rest, and I bounded back into bed. The bound made me cough. I spat – it tasted strange – it was bright red blood.*

I felt myself go pale.

You what? I said.

Since then I've gone on spitting each time I cough a little more, she said.

No, I said.

Perhaps it's going to gallop – who knows – she said, *and I shan't have my work written. That's what matters . . . unbearable . . . 'scraps', 'bits' . . . nothing real finished.*

I saw then how ill she looked, and how thin, and how far too young. I had to look away in case she saw, by looking at me, what I was seeing.

I began reading the songs in Twelfth Night in bed this morning early, she said.

Right, Twelfth Night, right, yes, I said.

Mark it, Cesario, it is old and plain. The spinsters and the knitters in the sun. And the free maids that weave their thread with bones. Do use to chant it – it is silly sooth. And dallies with the innocence of love. Like the old age, she said.

She saw how close to tears I was.

Come away, come away death, etc, she said.

Then she gave me a sly look from under her fringe.

I could make the girls cry when I read Dickens in the sewing class, she said.

*

And here it fell. Sepulchral.

That's the actual real line from the story you were telling me about once. I've read the story now. I've read all her stories, from the one at the start of the book where the girl is in the emptied house and the little birds flick from branch to branch, to the one at the end of her life about the poor bird in a cage, and that one about the fly that gets all inked. *Oh, the times when she had walked upside down on the ceiling, up, up glittering panes floated on a lake of light, flashed through a shining beam!*

I sat down in front of my computer in what was once our house and I typed the word WING into the subject heading. Then I wrote this.

Hello.

I wanted to tell you that I found out a thing that might be of use to you, well a couple of things, well three things altogether.

1: I was speaking to a lady from New Zealand at work because of our New Zealand contract and I told her I was reading your ex-wife and she told me an amazing story, and then she sent me a newspaper clipping, and this is what it says in short, that your ex-wife maybe was actually given birth to in a hot-air balloon. Yes I know it sounds unlikely and like I'm lying but I have the newspaper to prove it and I knew it would interest you. It says in it that her mother was pregnant with her and on the day your ex-wife was born she had actually booked to go up above Wellington in a balloon with a man called Mr Montgolf who was charging five shillings a shot. Anyway on 15 October 1888 a newspaper called The Dominion reported that the flight the day before took 'much longer than expected because of the medical condition of one of its female occupants . . . fortunately this young woman had recovered by the time the balloon landed'. Which means, the paper implies, that your ex-wife might have been born with both feet off the ground.

2: You know the story you told me about, the one with the word sepulchral in it? The one about the past-it lady who goes to act as an extra in films. Can you remember, I wonder, that there is a moment when she is filling in a form to see if she is the right sort of extra and it says, 'Can you aviate – high-dive – drive a car – buck-jump-shoot?' And you know how your ex-wife also did quite a lot of extra-work in films in the war years and once even caught a quite bad cold from doing a long shoot in evening dress in January? Well, I went looking for whether there was any chance of seeing her on any of these films, so far I have been unsuccessful. But I have discovered, by chance, that in the mid-1920s loads of those films, hundreds and hundreds of them made by the British film industry in the earlier years, were melted down and used to make the resin that was painted on the wings of aeroplanes to make them weather resistant. So now when you think of your ex-wife it is possible to think of those pictures of her moving as maybe really on the wing.

Also I remember that one of the things you were working on was a book by her friend and rival Virginia Woolf about a plane that all the people in London look up and see, that's writing words in the sky above them, and I remember you gave a paper about it somewhere. Well, I have deduced that because they started coating the wings of planes in or before 1924 with melted films, it is perfectly possible that the wings of the plane all those people are craning their necks and looking up at in Virginia Woolf's famous novel which if I am right is the one that was published in 1925, could actually be coated in melted-down moving pictures of your ex-wife. It is funny to me too because I have a sense that Virginia Woolf always thought your ex-wife a bit flighty.

3: Finally did you know that it is now possible to fly from Auckland to Sydney in your ex-wife? There is a new generation Boeing 737 that Qantas use whose features include a 12 seat business class and 156 seat economy, with individual state of the art Panasonic in-flight entertainment-on-demand systems in both business and economy, ergonomic cushions and adjustable headrests and a choice on board of New Zealand or Australian wines. The plane is called The Katherine Mansfield.

It all really makes me think of the thing she says where she says: 'Your wife won't have a tomb – she'll have at most a butterfly fanning its wings on her grave and then off.'

You might say I have been thinking of you a bit.

I very much hope you are well.

*

I didn't send that flight email in the end. I looked at my language and couldn't. I knew I'd got punctuation and things wrong, and was embarrassed at the words I'd used when I looked back at it later after a glass of wine, which is usually when embarrassment disappears and it's easier to press send. Those are some of the reasons I didn't send it.

The main one, though, was that I didn't want you to think I was trying to know more about something you knew about than you did. Also, I was worried that maybe you really wouldn't know these things. I realized I really didn't want to know more about what you knew about than you.

Which is all a roundabout way of saying I didn't want to trespass on what was yours.

Everything in life that we really accept undergoes a change.

So suffering must become love.

That is the mystery.

In the end what I did was this. The next time I was in London, I went to find the house your ex-wife had lived in for, well I didn't know if it was for longest, but I knew it was for happiest.

I stood outside it and I thought about how close it was to the Heath, and how much that must have pleased her cats. I worried about what an uphill climb it must have been to get to the house from the nearest Tube, for somebody not very well. I thought about how she wrote to this address from a cold house in Italy. She wrote imagining coming home and kissing its gate and door, and about how she imagined the cat going up the stairs, it was how she pictured home, and I think the word she used is *lopping, Wing come lopping up.* There's a big locked gate on it, too high to see over and you can't see in, though there is a blue plaque on it saying it is your ex-wife's house and that her husband lived there too. (The plaque doesn't mention the Mountain.) But I took a photo of the outside of it on my phone, and then I took a close-up of the brick of the whitewashed wall of it, where ivy or some plant with tiny splayed-out roots has grown over the place and someone has repeatedly stripped it back. Some of it, delicate, is preserved forever under the whitewash, and some of it has kept on growing new roots on top of the whitewash.

When I got home that night I keyed in your address above an email and sent you that photo of the wall and the plantlife without saying where it was of, or telling you anything about it.

Then I put the books I had stolen from you back on the shelf you'd kept them on in the study, and I shut the door. And then I went and got on with it, the rest of my life.

Here's a stanza from a poem by Jackie Kay called 'Dear Library', and this part I'm quoting is based on what her father, John Kay, said when she asked him what he thought about the public library system:

I treasure your lively silence; your very pleasant librarians.
They represent what a public service is truly, libertarian.
Impossible, did I say that already, to put a price on that. Again,
Stop me if I am repeating myself, your staff will tell
Me of a Saramago Street in a nearby town.
Browse, borrow, request, renew – lovely words to me.
A library card in your hand is your democracy.

Anna Ridley sent me this:

> *The local library of the Cumbrian market town where I lived provided plenty to satisfy my curiosity when I was growing up, with well-stocked children's and young adult sections. As I became a teenager, though, I needed more. Having experimented with Nietzsche, I got it into my mind I wanted to read the Marquis de Sade. I think I had read an interview with a musician in the* NME *who namechecked him or something. Finding nothing on the shelf, the kindly librarian, who had known me since I was born, checked the database. The only book that came up was* Justine, or Good Conduct Well Chastised, *which wasn't stocked in any of the local libraries, or even the city library – in fact there was only one copy in the whole county, and it was nearly ninety miles away. We filled out the request card and I waited. When the book arrived a few weeks later, it was a large hardback. I was alarmed as soon as I saw it – I can't remember exactly what was on the jacket, but I do remember it worried me enough that I bundled it straight into my school bag, and once I got home I removed the dust jacket and hid it behind my wardrobe. And having skimmed through the book and got the gist of it, even now it looked unassuming without its jacket, I hid it in a pile of books under my bed.*

I'm not sure what horrified me the most – the thought of my mum finding it, or the idea that the librarian had known all along what she was letting me in for! I'd like to say that age thirteen I'd read it, but actually after a few furtive encounters I kept it hidden under my bed until I came up with a cowardly plan to return it to the anonymous book drop in the bigger city library ten miles away. It amuses me to think of the miles that well-thumbed book had travelled, satisfying the curiosity of readers around the county, enabled by the library system. Not long afterwards, I got a Saturday job in a brilliant second-hand bookshop, from which I could borrow whatever I liked, and was able to pursue my reading curiosity a bit less publicly.

This is what Clare Jennings told me:

For me libraries represent a serendipity of learning. It's as if some internal compass draws you to areas which you never imagined visiting. At eighteen I started a degree in chemistry but didn't feel entirely at home in the subject and found myself repeatedly gravitating towards the small philosophy section in the library. Before the first year was out I'd left to study philosophy instead. I really enjoyed studying philosophy and while there found myself drawn to the art section of the library and later completed a second degree in illustration. Libraries can definitely lead you astray in the best possible way.

Emma Wilson sent me this:

In Jacques Rivette's 1974 film Céline and Julie Go Boating, Dominique Labourier plays a librarian. She has glasses as well as sexy shoes. This is a French library. You can smoke (discreetly). The librarians read the Tarot cards behind the desk with its stacked, ordered card index system. Juliet Berto, a magician, sits hiding behind a large size Bécassine picture book. The film plays in a Surrealist arcane. Its signs and titles point out to the streets of Montmartre.

In my local library in England when I was a child one of the librarians was French. I loved her. She made me feel she was intent just on me. Choosing books each week was like laying out the dreams I could have. I remember that beautiful moment of transition to borrowing from the adult section, the wider fan of cards, the longer shelves, a stretch of titles. And in that local library then, here in England, in the 1970s, there were books in French, lots of them, a whole case. I remember seeing the white and cream spines, the foreign words, lavish sentences, Colette, Duras.

I learnt to read those French books. In the library. Here in England.

Here's what Emily Wainwright and Lori Beck said:

Public libraries allow us to explore the self or the desired self in many forms

&

The only way I can express how important public libraries are is to tell you about myself.

And Natalie Williams sent me the following:

Once a week, on a Tuesday, a pale blue van would pull up outside the Post Office in the Dorset village I grew up in. The driver/librarian sitting behind her desk; the smell of slightly old and battered books in their plastic cases, the glue in their spines, the stamps in their inner sleeves. Four or so books every week, dutifully read and returned to the pale blue van on a Tuesday. It served as a precursor to when I was a little older and spent inordinate amounts of time at the Dorchester Library, which allowed a spectacular twelve withdrawals and had a brilliant biography and music section. I should add that we had plenty of books at home, but there was something about this weekly ritual that fuelled my love of books. I still have plenty of books at home, and I still sign up to my local library, regardless of where I am in the world.

The art of elsewhere

I've been trying to go elsewhere all my life.

Last year, I went all over the place. I went to Greece, I went to France, I went to Holland, I went to Morocco, I went to Canada, I went to Germany. That's just some of the places I went to. I flew, I cycled, I went on Eurostar, I went by ordinary train, I walked, I got the bus, I drove, I sat in the backs of a lot of taxis. Wherever I went, however I went, there was no getting away from it. I would put my bag down on the cobbles, or the pavement, or the grassy side of the road, or the walkway next to the canal, or the plastic-strewn beach, or the railway station platform, or the bed, or the folding table-thing made of canvas and aluminium that some hotels have especially for suitcases, and where would I be?

I'd be sitting on a bench in a pretty garden high up the side of a fairly built-up slope above the city of Naples. If you looked up you'd not see Vesuvius at all, because of the pollution. And if you looked down, you'd know Naples was down there, and you'd be able to hear the crazy hooting and roaring of the traffic, but because of the pollution it was like Naples didn't exist.

Beautiful.

I mean Rotterdam was lovely. It's got some great galleries. I particularly liked the medieval Madonna and Child with the tiny golden angels radiating out in interwoven rings round them both, playing golden musical instruments, forming a series of hoops of light, like vibrations or aura are emanating from them, and under her feet she's crushing a long thin black monstrous-looking thing, a kind of devil I suppose it's meant to be. And when I stood and looked at the painting, a painting as small as my own hand, of a pile of beautiful old books on a table and one book propped up and open at a double page, blank but for the figure of a man standing at the far end holding a spade, as if the blank pages were a field waiting to be farmed, for a moment, for a few seconds, looking at that picture, I was both right there in front of it and I was elsewhere.

Also, the gallery had a very lovely café/restaurant; there was leek soup the day I went, very nice, and even its toilets are works of art, with little plaques outside them like paintings have next to them for their title/artist information.

But pretty much the whole time I was there, I was still trying to get elsewhere.

*

There was a girl I knew when I was at school; her name was Debbie and her dad was famously elsewhere. That meant he was doing time, my mother told me; it was well known among the parents that Debbie's father, from time to time, did time. Her mother worked at the petrol station where my elder brother worked the car-wash on Saturdays and Sundays, and this, along with a kindly demeanour, meant that Debbie, who was quite a tough sort of girl, and the kind who failed exams or tended to do averagely, was protective of me if I ever came under threat from the little gangs of girls who'd hang around the school gates waiting to slap the face of a swot.

We had sewing class last thing on a Friday and for this we were seated alphabetically, which meant that Debbie and I were put next to each other. Because she knew I liked books she told me about her favourite book, which was The Railway Children by E. Nesbit. The film is good, yeah, she said, but the book is much, much better. Then she lent me it, and was so delighted, when I gave it back to her, that I'd liked it as much as she had that she actually did my sewing for me for weeks; she'd do her own double-quick then give me hers to hold, and work away at mine under the table, right under the sewing teacher's nose. It was the only term in my life that I ever got a good mark in sewing. Once, in an English class, our teacher, who called himself the Gaelic version of his name and was known for his ritual of firing a cannon and raising a saltire in his back garden every year at New Year, and who still wore a black gown to teach in, which no one else in the whole school did, and who always gave himself the best parts when we read Shakespeare round the class, and who despised Debbie for some reason, presumably because the staff, like the parents, knew about her dad and his doing time, told us all to open our poetry books at a poem by Rudyard Kipling called If. Then he said that the first one of us to stand up and recite, word-perfect, the whole thing off by heart could leave the class and go to lunch early.

It was the kind of cheap thing a teacher did when he didn't really want to teach the class that period. I thought about what I'd do with the time, if it was me who learned the words the fastest. Since there was nobody at home till one o'clock there'd be no point in me leaving school half an hour early, because I didn't have a key for the house and I'd have to sit in the garden until one of my parents got home from work, and the dog would hear me and start barking to get out, and anyway it was raining, but if the shed was unlocked, I could sit in the shed and wait. Okay.

But I had barely started reading the poem, barely got to the end of its second line, when someone at the back of the class pushed a chair back and stood up. We all turned.

Face the front, old Macneacail shouted.

Facing the front, we all heard Debbie begin at the beginning. If you can keep your head when all about you. Are losing theirs and blaming it on you. I followed the poem in the book in front of me through all four of its verses. She was word-perfect. She ended at the end. You'll be a man, my son, she said.

Then she picked up her bag and walked between the desks to the front of the class.

Ah, but you didn't learn that here in this classroom today, though, did you, em, eh, –, old Macneacail, who was flustered and had misplaced Debbie's name, said.

My father says it into the mirror every morning when he shaves, Debbie said. And you never said anything about us not being allowed to know it already.

She swung out the door without looking back. The door clicked shut. We were all left behind.

Debbie had gone elsewhere.

*

Elsewhere there are no mobile phones. Elsewhere sleep is deep and the mornings are wonderful. Elsewhere art is endless, exhibitions are free and galleries are open twenty-four hours a day. Elsewhere alcohol is a joke that everybody finds funny. Elsewhere everybody is as welcoming as they'd be if you'd come home after a very long time away and they'd really missed you. Elsewhere nobody stops you in the street and says, are you a Catholic or a Protestant, and when you say neither, I'm a Muslim, then says yeah but are you a Catholic Muslim or a Protestant Muslim? Elsewhere there are no religions. Elsewhere there are no borders. Elsewhere nobody is a refugee or an asylum seeker whose worth can be decided about by a government. Elsewhere nobody is something to be decided about by anybody. Elsewhere there are no preconceptions. Elsewhere all wrongs are righted. Elsewhere the supermarkets don't own us. Elsewhere we use our hands for cups and the rivers are clean and drinkable. Elsewhere the words of the politicians are nourishing to the heart. Elsewhere charlatans are known for their wisdom. Elsewhere history has been kind. Elsewhere nobody would ever say the words bring back the death penalty. Elsewhere the graves of the dead are empty and their spirits fly above the cities in instinctual, shapeshifting formations that astound the eye. Elsewhere poems cancel imprisonment. Elsewhere we do time differently.

Every time I travel, I head for it. Every time I come home, I look for it.

This is what Kamila Shamsie told me about why libraries, and what becomes of libraries, matter:

> *The library was located on Bleak House Road. It had high ceilings, and whirring fans and thick brick walls painted light blue which kept both paper and humans from curling over in the Karachi heat. Those were the days of military dictatorship when the movie 'Rambo III' (in which the hero killed Soviets in Afghanistan) seemed to be the only cultural import that the state deemed necessary for its citizens; some English language bookshops did exist but they were likely to stock primarily the kinds of novel that I would later learn to refer to as 'airport bestsellers' rather than anything that conformed to my childhood tastes. Besides, my reading rate of a*

book a day would have made it impossible for bookstores alone to meet my needs, even if we weren't in Rambo world.

And so, the visits to the British Council library on Bleak House Road where, if memory serves, a single pink library card allowed you to withdraw six books at a time. I read my way from childhood to adolescence here – Rumpole of the Bailey left me cold, but Mary Renault's Alexander trilogy was everything I wanted from fiction. That I remember those grim days of dictatorships as personally filled with joy and possibility has more than a little to do with the thrill of a library where it was possible to encounter the whole world from Alexander the Great to the newest version of me (for what better way to mark the changes in yourself than via the books your eyes once skipped over which now hold you in their thrall?).

In 2002, post 9/11 'security concerns' shut down the library. It has yet to re-open. Talk to Karachi's citizens long enough about what that vast, troubled city of 20 million plus most needs and eventually you stumble on the phrase 'places to escape to'. In other words, libraries.

After life

Ten years ago it was reported in the Evening News that I was dead. LOCAL MAN DIES.

We were in Spain on holiday. When we got home the neighbours came running out to meet us. LOCAL MAN NOT DEAD AFTER ALL.

The paper apologized profusely, sent flowers. I became a minor celebrity. I'd be walking down the street and total strangers would cross the road to shake my hand. I went in to work the following Monday; it was really something, coming back from the dead. Several women even made advances (and I showed them both, well, the one who definitely did, my wedding ring; I am an old-fashioned kind of man at the end of the day).

I'd get home and my wife, Ellie, would kiss me and mean it; our two kids would look at me like I was a king. We held a dinner party for all our friends; we fitted our twenty-eight guests all the way up the stairs in the house and took a group photo with the camera delay button. It was a wonderful night. And the next night Ellie and I sat back into the sofa and watched Top of the Pops and Annie Lennox was on, battleworn but undaunted; she was going to be one of the people singing the new Millennium in. Our two kids cuddled into us, my wife was pregnant. Death wasn't relevant to me.

Then, yesterday, ten years almost to the day, it happens again. LOCAL MAN DIES.

The report says I was hit in my Mazda by a truck at a road junction, that the truck had been delivering online shopping and that its driver suffered minor injuries.

I phone the police to tell them I'm not dead and that I don't have and have never had a Mazda. They tell me they've no record of me being dead anyway. I phone the paper. I leave a voice message on an automated phone system, which instructs me that the best way to contact them is online. I knock on Chloe's bedroom door. Chloe flings the door open. She's the only person in this house who opens a door fully these days.

How can I be of subsistence? she says.

Can I use your computer? I say. Your brother and sister are using theirs, and your mother's looking up Michael Ball on ours.

Mitch is using mine, she says.

Chloe, I say.

He's helping me do a genealogy search, she says.

You're nearly ten, I say. Stop it.

You can use it –, she says.

Thank you, I say.

– but only if you acknowledge Mitch, she says.

Mitch has been a figment of Chloe's imagination for about four months now. His full name is Mitchell Kenyon. Chloe has somehow come by a DVD of some ancient silent films, just of ordinary everyday people, made by two men called Mitchell and Kenyon a hundred years ago. The films were almost thrown in a skip but now they're golddust and film buffs are restoring them. I know all this because Chloe watched the DVD obsessively on the lounge DVD player until I complained about wanting to watch TV. Mitch is what she's decided to call the small boy she's seen in one, got a crush on, and claimed as companion as surely as if he'd rolled bodily out of one of those old metal cans himself and turned up at our house. When I asked her a couple of weeks ago how old he was, she thought for a moment then said, a hundred and eighteen. I'm putting my foot down, he's far too old for you, I said. That's quite witty, Dad, she said. It's like going out with your great-grandfather, I said. Did I ever tell you the story of your great-grandfather and the jungle? Uh huh, how he was in a war, Chloe said, and they made a road, they cut through the jungle to make it, and the next morning they woke up and the road they'd made had disappeared, the jungle grew back over it overnight, lots of times, and I'm not going out with Mitch, we're just friends. What, like your mother's three hundred and fourteen Michael Ball Fan friends on Facebook? I said. The difference is, Chloe said, that Mum's belief that they're her friends *is* a figment of the imagination.

I contact the Evening News by phone and email that night. But in the morning the online report is still pronouncing me dead. So before I go to work, and because the phone won't connect me to anyone alive, I go in person to the newspaper offices. I speak to someone upstairs in editorial through a security speaker system downstairs outside the front door of the building.

It says here James Gerard is deceased, the box-voice says.

I'm him, I say.

I've just checked it again and with all due respect, the voice says.

Something catches my eye through the reinforced glass of the door. A CCTV black bubble in the ceiling of their foyer is blinking a red light at me.

Can you see me? I say.

I wave.

Have you got photographic proof of ID? it says.

I get my driver's licence out and slap it against the glass.

We'll need a verification meeting with the newsgroup's lawyers and your own self's lawyers present before we can take this discussion any further, it says.

Is this a joke? I say.

The tannoy system clicks off. I hit the doorbell speaker box with the flat of my hand. Two security men appear from nowhere and stare at me through the reinforced glass. I mouth the words I'm not dead at them.

Then I go to work.

I'm alive again, then, I say to Claudine on reception.

Right, Claudine says.

She is slumped at her desk, her face pale in the light off her screen, her chin in her hand like it's the end of the day. It's 9.15 a.m.

I circulate the report of my death in an email headed You Only Live Thrice. My computer spellcheck asks me did I mean You Only Live The Rice. I get one email back. *Amazing*, it says, *wow. Can you copy me the file re Friday's meeting and confirm the confirmation?* Nobody phones. Nobody makes a pass at me.

When I get home not a single person has phoned the landline about whether I am alive or dead, though there are two cold-call messages on the answerphone from double glazing life assurance salespeople.

I sit beside Ellie at the dining room table.

Clearly there's no story in coming back to life, I say.

Mm, she says.

Why has this happened twice to me, d'you think? I say.

Really strange, Ellie says.

She doesn't take her eye off the screen.

Can I use the laptop? I say.

I'm busy on it, Ellie says.

Yeah, but all you're doing is looking up pictures of koalas, I say.

She turns and glares at me.

Chlamydia. Eucalyptus shortage. Drought. The koalas are *dying*, she says. And there's nothing we can *do*.

There is desperation in her eyes. I look away. I don't say anything. Then I go upstairs.

I stand outside Nathan's room. At Hallowe'en a boy in the same school year as him was kicked to real death by three sixteen-year-olds outside a kebab shop, apparently because he was wearing gloves.

The door is shut. Foreign-sounding music is playing in his room. I knock.

He's watching Euro porn, Emily shouts through her own shut bedroom door. He needs cognitive behavioural therapy for being fascistly satisfied like the rest of the brainless masses by brainless wank and if he wanks in the upstairs bathroom again I'll tell all the girls in his class what he does all night, the wanker.

Emily, I say to her door. Don't use words like that in this house.

Which ones? she shouts back.

Cognitive, behavioural and therapy, I say.

Chloe opens her door.

I think I can be of persistence, she says.

I look up the Evening News website on Chloe's computer and find that news of my death has been syndicated to all local news sources and has also spread to 1,663 sites. The response piece I sent last night saying I'm actually alive is published in their 'Opinions' blogspace. Below it is a post from someone called sophiecatxyz who castigates *whoever is pretending to be James Gerard a man who has clearly died tragically* for causing *pain and emotional upset to a grieving family*. Below this someone called Doctormyeyes has written: *Like Michael Jacskon he may be dead but he will never ever die*. I click on a link to a blog by someone called truthizoutther who says I'm *definitely dead as a dodu as a doornail his coast is toast RIP JAME GERARD dead meat accept it man only zombies fight the force submit ok?? lol.*

I fill in the little reply box. At least I'm more alive

than you are, I write. At least I can spell dodo properly, something you're clearly too braindead to do.

I sign my name. I thwack the send icon. I immediately feel better. Then I feel much worse and wish I hadn't sent anything to anyone. It is somehow a defeat to have engaged at all.

Chloe is playing with a plastic pony on her bed. She is galloping it up to a ridge in the covers and making it jump over the ridge. Each time she makes the ridge a little higher. I watch her form with her hands and knees a particularly high ridge.

Chloe, I say. Am I dead?

We are certain that you are not dead, she says.

Who? I say. You and the horsie?

I'm not a child, she says. You know perfectly well who.

Chloe, I say. You've been told.

She squares the pony in front of the high wall of bedspread and duvet. Then she starts pressing buttons on her phone.

Who are you texting at this time of night? I say.

My pony, to wish him luck, she says.

Does your pony have a mobile? I say.

Dad, she says as if the word dad means stupid.

What about Rip Van Mitchell? I say. Does he have one?

Chloe shakes her head.

It's like when the one eyed giant shut the sailor in

the cave and started eating his shipmates, she says, and the sailor has to think how to get them all out of there, and what they do is they sharpen the phone mast and they stick it right in its eye.

What, like with the Cyclops? I say.

And then they camouflage themselves and get out of there, Chloe says. Because there's so much more of the journey still to go. But they have to be ingenious to survive. He has to be a nobody. I'm A Nobody, Get Me Out Of Here. Do you want to stay for the Puissance?

The what? I say. Are you doing the Cyclops at school?

Half horse, half bike, Chloe says. Mitch thinks that humans will evolve like in Charles Darwin to have a square screen in our foreheads instead of having eyes. We will look at their screen to see everything we need to know. We won't need to cogitate any more.

Enough of the Mitching, I say.

Are you finished on my MacBook? she says. Put it here. No, closed. It's the water jump.

It takes me a while to get it. Cyclops: half horse, half bike. When I finally do I'm in bed, lying awake again next to my sleeping wife. I'd come downstairs and she'd been looking up the symptoms of diseases. Why? I said. To see if I've got any of them, she said. Are you feeling unwell? I asked. She looked at me in surprise. No, she said, not at all.

I get out of bed and put my dressing gown on. I stand for five minutes in the dark. I look out of the window at the front gardens of our neighbours in the streetlight, at the way the light reflects off the roofs of all our cars.

Then I shake Ellie awake. I bang on all the bedroom doors. I tell everybody to meet me round the dining room table. I put the kettle on. I look in the fridge. There are some olives, grapes. I slice a carrot into sticks and upend a tub of hummus on to a plate. I open a bottle of wine.

As soon as she gets into the living room Emily presses the TV remote.

Put it off, Emily, I say.

I'm watching it, she says.

Turn it down, I say.

She turns it fractionally down and angles her chair away from the table towards it. As the rest of them come downstairs bleary, the Twin Towers erupt again onscreen and I remember seeing it for the first time, I was passing a TV shop in town and every screen was showing the same thing. A programme called The Top One Hundred Things You Need To Know About The Noughties is on. A fast edit montage flashes up images of the Cheeky Girls, a MySpace page, a broadband hub, a page of Tesco's online site, a newscaster with the words WMD on the screen behind her, Tony Blair laughing, the boys who present I'm A Celebrity in the jungle, an iPod, the word Twitter, a melting icecap, the painted C of the Congestion Charge, people holding little plastic bags in departures, a copy of The Da Vinci Code, the logo for YouTube, a newspaper hoarding saying MPS EXPENSES DUCKPOND SCANDAL, Damien Hirst's skull, some logos for banks, Kirsty and Phil, people being vaccinated by a doctor in a surgery, Andy Murray flexing his arm-muscles, a PowerBook, a contestant for Big Brother coming out to a booing crowd, the screen of an iPhone, Baghdad in flames, a bendy bus.

The decade between my deaths.

I make Chloe put the extra chair for Mitch back where it was, against the wall.

The kids look exhausted. My wife looks at the food on the table and the full glass of wine by her hand. She looks at me with tiredness and suspicion.

I just thought we should all, you know, talk, I say.

It's half past two in the morning. What do you want to talk about? she says.

Anything you like, I say.

She looks away.

I look at my son.

Nathan? I say.

I mime taking earphones out of my ears. He does as I ask.

Start the conversation, son, I say. Anything.

Anything random. Tell us what you were doing earlier this evening.

Ha ha! Emily says.

Nathan has gone bright red. I change the subject, quick.

Tell us about what *you* think has most changed over the last ten years, I say. The difference between then and now.

The indifference between then and now, he means, Emily says.

Nathan looks wasted. He is far too thin and as dark-eyed as his mother. I realize it's now the norm for him to look as though he's permanently flinching.

It isn't porn, he says.

He looks straight at Emily.

It's bike gear systems, he says. It's fourteen, twenty-one, twenty-seven gear systems and speed hubs.

That's crap, Emily says. I saw. You were watching a porn movie with a gang bang in a prison.

I was not, he says. That's a YouTube clip of a film star in a foreign film where she goes to prison by mistake and in the cell these men crowd round her and sing a song. And she is really beautiful, and innocent. I don't mean innocent in a perv way, I mean innocent of the crime she is put in prison for.

He has gone bright red from the neck to the roots

of his hair. But he stands up decisively, pushes his chair back, stands up, leaves the room.

Geek, Emily says without taking her eye off the TV.

Emily, that's enough, Ellie says.

Yeah, well, if he can go to bed so can I, she says. And the difference between then and now is that *now* I'm supposed to wear clothes that make me look like a prostitute and if I don't I'm not a proper girl. And *now* it's okay to be friends with Hana at school and everything but out in the world I'm supposed to think she's one of them not us and that her family are them not us too and that if her big brother isn't a terrorist already then it's only a matter of time.

She switches the TV off on her way out.

My wife stands up. She stares at the off screen.

The difference, she says in the after-TV silence, is that over the last ten years new communication technology has brought people so much closer together.

She gives no sign that she's joking. She picks up as many of the things on plates as she can carry, backs out of the room, lets the door fall shut behind her. I hear her putting things away in the fridge. Then I hear her going slowly upstairs.

Chloe has her head down on her arm on the table. Her eyes are shut.

What about you? I say.

The difference between then and now, is, Chloe says. I wasn't here then, and now I am.

A moment later she's asleep. I look at the top of her head, at the way her hair knows to shape itself. I pick her up and shoulder her, carry her upstairs, tuck her in.

On my way out of her room I see the beloved DVD on the computer desk. I take it with me and go back downstairs.

I turn the sound down low.

These films are all from the first decade of the last century, the voice-over tells me. They were throwaways, made for a quick buck. It's a miracle they still exist. 'Local Films For Local People.' 'Come And See Yourself On The Screen As Living History!' They'd be made in the afternoon and shown that same night in touring fairs or theatres, and the filmmakers would cram as many local faces in as possible so the number of people paying to see themselves would be maximum too.

I switch the voice-over off so I can see better. The first years of the last century flicker away in silence. The films are of happy-looking crowds, schoolyards full of children demonstrating to the camera how healthy and happy they are, workers waving and smiling. There's quite a bit of poverty. But in film after film of seaside promenades, football matches, people in hats at Whitsun, people at fairs, people rolling Easter eggs down hills, the hundreds and hundreds of dead working people wave their hats and handkerchiefs in circles in the air, wave at the camera, at themselves. The children are especially curious and excited. It strikes me they'll be cannon fodder for Ypres and the Somme in just a decade's time.

I get to a film made in North Shields in 1901. It begins with hardy-looking girl-fishgutters, a shot of boats, a large crowd gathered round a harbour. Then, in among the people, a small boy in a flat cap notices the camera and turns towards it as if towards me, here, now, more than a century later sitting in this room of empty chairs in the middle of the night. He resembles Chloe slightly. He disappears out of frame, then ducks back in. That's what she'd do. He doesn't wave. He isn't delighted. He's questioning, grave. He means business. He wants to know. There is no other way to put it: he is completely alive. The life in him pierces me.

He is ten years old at the turn of a new century and less than a minute long. For as many of those seconds as he gets the chance to, he looks the future in the eye. He walks towards it, holding its eye steady in both of his.

Eve Lacey spoke to me about the way books carry their histories, and about the new history of public libraries.

She's the current Library Graduate Trainee at Newnham College Library in Cambridge; she'd previously worked in a public library in one of the local villages, a fairly well-heeled place, though even there, she said, the most vulnerable really need and use the library, the homeless and jobless people, along with a real mixture of all the generations, especially elderly people and young mothers with children. She told me about the pressure on the public library service to move from council funding to volunteer status, about the way the community there has rushed to protect and sustain the library, about the inevitable catch-22 downgrading situation when something shifts from public funding to less or no funding, and about the official council letters that circulated concerning desperate money-saving tactics ('a 1 per cent reduction in pay would save approximately £1.28 million . . . therefore a 2.4 per cent reduction the necessary £3 million savings . . . one day of unpaid leave would save £0.4 million . . . the withdrawal of pay increments for the year would save approx. £1.4 million . . . stopping the first day of sick pay could save approx. £0.5 million and stopping the first two days £0.8 million').

She told me about the unbelievable length of the queue of excited local children taking part in the Summer Reading Challenge there, a literacy-encouraging initiative where a child reads a book a week then comes back and tells the librarian about the book; she said the line of children wanting to talk about the books they'd read stretched out the door.

She told me about why the Rare Books Rooms in libraries keep books at a certain temperature – because the leather which binds early books is always trying to get back to the original shape of the animal whose skin it was, and the temperature regulation keeps it book-shape. She told me that 250 Bibles bound in calf leather generally equalled 250 actual calves. She told me that the gilt on the edges of books has antiseptic properties, being part gold, and dust-repelling properties. Proper gilding cleans itself.

Then she and the Librarian, Debbie Hodder, took me through into the stacks of the college library (a library formed against all the odds in the late 1800s – the women who studied at Cambridge, which didn't admit women as full members of the University till 1948, weren't permitted to use or access the University's books; the library is, more than a century later, one of the best-stocked college libraries in the city). They showed me a lock of Charlotte Brontë's hair coiled inside a ring, told me the library also happens to hold in its collection a tennis dress of the 1890s which looks like it would be incredibly heavy to wear, and they let me see several books, including one called An Elementary Treatise on Curve Tracing, by Percival Frost (1892), which begins: In order to understand this work on the tracing of curves whose equations are given in Cartesian coordinates, all that is required of the student is that he shall know the ordinary rules of Algebra as far as the Binomial theorem, the fundamental theorems of the Theory of Equations, and the general methods employed in Algebraic Geometry.

Inside the front cover of this book there are a couple of pasted-in notices. On the left-hand inside page, the notice reads:

1917
BRITISH PRISONERS
INTERNED ABROAD
This book is the gift of Miss M. Fletcher
Newnham College Cambridge
and is supplied through the Agency
at the Board of Education
Whitehall London S. W.

On the right-hand inside page, the pasted-in note says in clear handwriting:

If this book is ever returned,
it will be gratefully received,
though not expected.
M. Fletcher, Librarian
Newn: Coll: Cambridge
Jan 1917.

Underneath that, it says, in the same hand:

Returned May 13, 1919.

The definite article

I stepped out of the city and into the park. It was as simple as that.

It was January, it was a foggy day in London town, I'd got off the Tube at Great Portland Street and come up and out into the dark of the day, I was on my way to an urgent meeting about funding. It was possible in the current climate that funding was going to be withdrawn so we were having to have an urgent meeting urgently to decide on the right kind of rhetoric. This would ensure the right developmental strategy which would in turn ensure that funding wouldn't conclude in this way at this time. I had come the whole way underground saying over and over in my head, urgent, ensure, feasibility, margin, assessment, management, rationalization, developmental strategy, strategic development, current climate, project incentive, core values, shouldn't conclude, in this way, at this time. But it also had to be unthreatening, the language we were to use to ensure etc, so I went up the stairs repeating to myself the phrase not a problem not a problem not a problem, then stopped for a moment at the Tube exit because (ow) my eye was really hurting, out of nowhere I'd got something in my eye.

It made everything else disappear. I stopped and stood. I blinked. I felt about in one of my pockets, folded the edge of a kleenex into what felt like a point and ran it along the inside of my lower lid. I blinked again and looked to see. The something that had been in my eye was stuck now on the edge of the kleenex. It was tiny, and it might once have had legs, hard to tell now. Maybe its legs were still in my eye; the eye was still stinging a little, still running. Running. Legs. Ha ha.

Urgent. Core values. Shouldn't conclude.

The eye was still a bit sore. I tried focusing into the distance. What I saw was the edge of the park. Then I saw myself pressing the button on the pedestrian crossing. Then I was crossing the road anyway, between the fast-coming cars, before I changed my mind.

On the wide path on Avenue Gardens I dried a bit of bench with the kleenex I still had in my hand. I sat down and held my other hand over the sore eye. I could hear traffic, background, faded. When my eye stopped stinging, I'd go back.

But it was turning into one of the days in January that spring sends ahead of itself. The fog would burn off. It was burning off right now. It was clearing. I could see. There were magpies. There were pigeons. There were all sorts of birds, everywhere. When was the last time I had looked at a blackbird, or at a robin? When was the last time I had looked properly at anything? There were runners on the park's paths. There was a cordon of very young schoolchildren out on a trip in the middle of the day. There was a man whistling, walking along holding a can of Skol ahead of himself. He was holding the can like a compass. There was a man in a wheelchair, being wheeled by a boy. The boy looked very like him. There was a man with a camera on a tripod. He was filming a woman who'd stopped to feed a squirrel. There was a woman doing a sideways-stepping walking exercise. There were two joggers and a dog. The dog, keeping the pace beside them, looked full of happiness, and there were patterns everywhere, in the line of benches stretching towards and away from me, in the fountains and the stone urns, in the trees, in the died-back tidied beds of flowers, and that's when I remembered something I hadn't thought about in years, it's back when I'm twenty-five, we've been together for six weeks, we've no money, it's my birthday and as a birthday present you sit me down and blindfold me. You lead me by the hand, blindfolded, out of the flat to where your old Mini with the holes in its floor is parked. You guide me into the car and then you drive me I have no idea where. There's a strangeness in every noise. Everything I touch and everything that touches me is so complex that all my senses flare. How closed-in things are when we're in the car, and is this what open actually means, when you get me out of it, still blindfolded, and lead me up a steep path, into what feels like somewhere whose openness will never end? At the top of this steepness we stop. You take me by the shoulders and turn me. You wish me happy birthday. Then you take the blindfold off me.

It's light, colour, it's the top of the hill. It's the city itself I see under the huge sky.

It was one of the best birthday presents I'd ever been given, I knew now so many birthdays on, twenty-five years later, a different person yet the same person, sitting in the park in the future, one hand over one eye. Where were you now? I wondered. What were you doing right now in the world?

A bee passed me. It was quite a large bee, bright yellow and black. A bee in January? Far too early in the year for a bee to be out, it should be wintering, it would surely die. I'd better go, I thought. I had a (not a problem) meeting to chair, and as clear as day the thought came into my head. I could follow that bee up Avenue Gardens. I could turn left and go to the Rose Garden. I hadn't been to the Rose Garden for years. There'd surely be some roses out, regardless of January, and I could go and see the little statue of Cupid with his arrows, was I remembering rightly, riding on the back of a stone duck or a goose? Cupid, with the tips of his arrows dipped in honey. And what was that old poem, about Cupid getting stung by a bee and complaining to his mother, Venus, and her holding her sides laughing at him because of the stings his arrows give lovers, and him put out by a tiny bee? Cupid, in a bed of roses, no, Cupid, as he lay among, Roses by a bee got stung.

It was years since I'd thought of that poem.

It was years since I'd thought about any poem.

I would go and look at the little statue to see if Cupid really was sitting on the back of a bird, or if I was just imagining it. When I'd done that I could go to the meeting.

Urgent. The word was a bit shaming when I thought about it. Not a problem. What did not a problem actually mean?

I would go to the Rose Garden. From there I would walk to the boating lake, then up past the sports pitches to the big fountain and round by the zoo.

From there I'd go to the bottom of Primrose Hill, choose a path, any path, and follow it to the top.

*

That was all, the passing thought, the mere slant of the thought of all the different possible ways there are just to cross a park, and that did it, the morning shook its pelt, slipped its rein and did a sideways dash across Regent's Park – no, not just Regent's Park but *the* Regent's Park, *the* park, the park that began as a forest whose sky was the tops of its trees, then the park of the left-handed King on horseback chasing the stag (and that's why the park is the lopsided shape it is, because Henry the Eighth was left-handed, so when he drew over the map of the Abbess's woods to mark the land he wanted *thus*, that's what his hand did, made a great curve there and a straight line there). The park of grazing smutty sheep (it's Henry James who called them smutty), the park of visions and assignations, fairs and ballads, footpads in their element, prostitutes in their ribbons. The park of the pretty girl out walking among the pretty flowers, taken suddenly and kissed hard on the mouth, *pray, alarm yourself not, Madame, you can now boast you've been kissed by Dick Turpin*. The park with the roofless theatre, A Midsummer Night's Dream in the midsummer air. The park where the crowds fed as much cake and biscuit as they could to Jumbo, The

Biggest Elephant In The World, who'd been sold to America, in the hope it'd make him too heavy to be shipped across the Atlantic.

First it was Cromwell felling the trees for the Navy, *534 acres with 124 deer and 16,297 tree of oak, ash, elm, wite thorn and maple.* Then it was Nash, deciding what new trees to use, pairing the colours of different kinds of tree to suit his villas. Then they felled the trees all over again for the twentieth-century wars. More than three hundred bombs changed the shape of the place in the 1940s. And now it's now. The park that began with the lords and the ladies in their carriages. The park that evolved, that learned to open its gates to everybody, to hold all the city's hundreds of languages, the city's efflorescence, in the one place. *Great forest of wooded glades*; the first written description we have of the Forest of Middlesex, which became the Great Chase, the Marrowbone, the Marybone, the Marylebone Pleasure Gardens, the Marylebone Park, the Regent's Park, where today, like any old day of the week, the day in the park curved itself off like a bird into the air over the six thousand trees, the laughable colours of duck, the black swans in the Rose Garden drinking the earlier drizzle off their own backs, all the people on their way to work who love to walk through the park, the young couple slowing their pace for their old slow dog on the Broad Walk, the man shouting at the woman cyclist and the cyclist giving him the perfectly reversed V sign over her shoulder, the magpies gathering in wait for feeding time over the zoo's walls, the Primrose Hill bookshop where stray leaves from the park blow in at the door all year round.

The day in the park, like any old day, took its usual bee-line, one never threatened by mere winter (which only makes the fountains more beautiful, the ice forming all down the sides of them), one that always makes something of itself, like the honey the Regent's Park bees make of their visits to the lime trees in Avenue Gardens, or the honey that tastes of roses in the seasons when the Rose Garden proves good pickings for the bees. Amber Queen. English Miss. Wandering Minstrel. Sweet Dreams. Ingrid Bergman. Anna Ford. Mayor of Casterbridge. Old Yellow Scotch. There are hives all over the park where, right now, the bees would be crowding together to keep the temperature up, would be taking turns to be circled and warmed by all the other bees, would be tending to the year's future bees in their cells; there are beehives in good quiet places all over the park.

Look at that, nothing but a passing honeybee, the kind of nothing that has two sets of eyes and makes a thousand flower-visits a day, a creature so clever that bees are already teaching themselves to combat the mites and diseases that have been killing them off so rapidly and so mysteriously (to humans at least) over the past few years. What's honey? A sweetener? Two pounds of honey equals a hundred thousand bee miles. The ancient Egyptians were the first to use it as an antiseptic, it's good on a burn, and it's not just good with a cough or a sore throat, it can help fight anthrax, diphtheria, cholera, MRSA, and when doctors transplant people's corneas the replacements are transported in honey.

Without bees? Nothing. Nothing pollinated. Hardly any fruit, almost no vegetables. All the food chains disrupted, from the human one down to the insect.

The beekeeper's got twenty-eight hives in the park at the moment. He has no idea if they'll survive the winter. Last year in the park only five out of twenty hives survived, and the year that followed was rough; a too-warm February, a too-cold spring, a too-wet summer; the bees needed supplementary feeding, God knows what's to come. He began with imported New Zealand queens; they're pretty, bright yellow and black. He's worked at creating new colonies, new queens, in case of the same kind of bee loss as last year.

Urgent. Current climate. He works for no salary. He makes a tiny profit on the honey he sells. Local feral bees are much blacker in colour. Last year he saw the yellow of the bees foraging in the roses by the café in the Inner Circle and he knew immediately they were Regent's Park's bees. The spring honey tasted, last year, of lime and somehow of passionfruit. Does light have a taste? Does the park have a taste? The late-extraction honey last year was medicinal, sweet, dark and powerful.

Could any place be more historied and less ghostly? Where's the ghost of the poet Elizabeth Barrett stealing the park's flowers to put in an envelope addressed to her fiancé, Robert, in Italy? Where are the ghosts of Percy Bysshe Shelley and Mary Shelley, sailing their paper boats on the pond? Where are the ghosts of the forty-odd people who went skating in January in 1867 and drowned in the lake when the ice gave way? Even them, cold and shivering, with the right to be a bit aggrieved, the right to hang about complaining for over a century, they're just not here. It's all open air. There's nothing dead and gone about it. Elizabeth Bowen, watching the swans *in their slow indignation*; and Richard Wagner standing at the lake throwing bread to the ducks; and Samuel Johnson causing a mini riot because it's too wet for the fireworks he's come to see; Charles Dickens, melancholy, a woman's been drowned in the canal; old George Bernard Shaw young again on the seat of a far-too-fast bike; Dodie Smith filling the park with the imaginary barks of dogs; Sylvia Plath, real as can be, hearing the hungry lion roar over the crib of her newborn child; then Ted Hughes, newly bereaved, the zoo-wolf howl in his ears; and Virginia Woolf herself, howling or furious or sad, doesn't matter which, walking and walking by the flower-beds till it cheers her up, leaves her happily *making up phrases*.

There's the woman who comes into the park at half past six in the morning and spends all the daylight hours leaving little mounds of cake and sunflower seeds (she always buys organic) in the same places so the wildlife will find it there when it comes looking.

There's the story of the man who, nearly two hundred years ago, bought four tiny birds from a sailor he met in the park. He put the birds in his pocket. When he got back to his lodgings he set the birds free. He watched them soar up over London.

Bet you any money, even if they'd been snared there in the first place, those birds flew straight back to the park.

*

One entire Park, compleat in unity of character. Endless stories, all crossing across each other, and mine tiny, negligent, quick as a blink, where nothing much happened except this: I stepped out of myself and into the park, I stepped off the pavement and into a place where there's never a conclusion, where regardless of wars, tragedies, losses, finds, the sting or the sweetness of what's gone in a life, or the preoccupations of any single time, any single being, on it goes, the open-air theatre of flowers, trees, birds, bees.

In this way, at this time, nothing concluded.

In other words: in foggy London town the sun, shining everywhere. The meeting could wait. It did wait, while I sat on the bench in Avenue Gardens and thought about the poem where the god of love gets stung by a bee and his mother laughs at him, and about whether there were as many different kinds of rose in the Rose Garden as there were different languages spoken in the city of London, and about the day back then when a visit to the park gave me back my own senses.

I had no idea where you were today in the world. But I remembered, sitting there in the park, what it meant that our paths had crossed. I remembered, too, that old Mini you had and how its floor had rusted right through, and how we could look down and see the surface of the road pass so quickly beneath us that going at thirty miles per hour, twenty, ten, even something near walking-pace, shocked me every time with what it was that words like fast or slow or road or city really meant.

Urgent. Core values. When I got cold I walked across the park in the happy noise of blackbirds. Then I went to the top of the hill and looked at the view. The city gathered round the park and rose out of itself as usual. I saw it all over again, as if for the first time.

*

Cupid, as he lay among
Roses, by a Bee was stung.
Whereupon in anger flying
To his Mother, said thus crying:
Help! O help! your Boy's a dying.
And why, my pretty Lad, said she?
Then blubbering replyed he,
A winged Snake has bitten me,
Which country people call a Bee.
At which she smil'd; then with her hairs
And kisses drying up his tears:
Alas! said she, my Wag! if this
Such a pernicious torment is:
Come, tel me then, how great's the smart
Of those, thou woundest with thy Dart!

(from Anacreon, translated by Robert Herrick)

Miriam Toews told me about how once, a couple of years ago, when she was sitting reading at a desk in Toronto's public library, she saw her own mother come in and sit down in one of the sunlit seats by the windows. Her mother, without noticing her daughter there, settled down, stretched out and fell asleep.

She sat where she was and watched her mother sleep.

A library assistant approached her mother. She saw this assistant reach out a tentative hand and give her mother a shake.

Her mother didn't wake up.

The assistant stepped back, stood as if thinking about it for a moment, then left her mother sleeping in the library sunlight.

Grass

I am no longer as young. But it's May, chilly and damp but May. That sound above the far-off noise of traffic is birds. That smell is cow parsley. It's rife in the hedgerow all round me now. A couple of hours ago when I was stuck on the motorway and hedgerows weren't even imaginable, the air that came into the car was high with the smell of something, and when I finally got off the main road and on to the back roads I found out what.

My car is near worthless. It's worth so much less than I imagined that the fact that it still works at all is now surprising to me. I'd taken it to the dealership two towns away, took it to market like in Jack and the Beanstalk when he takes the cow to sell because they're so poor they have to give up the last thing of value they own. I'd been in a traffic jam all the way back: a pile-up further along the motorway; it wasn't the accident itself that was causing the crawl but the fact that everybody who drove past it slowed up to take phone footage. Nothing was moving. So I pressed the window button, which works very well in my worthless car, and I leaned out. I played with the channels on the radio and the button that makes the surroundsound happen. I switched the radio off. I checked my eyes in the mirror. I checked my teeth. I checked my phone. I noticed that the car clock was still on winter time. (This explained why I'd been exactly an hour late for a couple of meetings over the past few months.) I pressed the button that changes time. Summer at last. We inched forward then came to a standstill. I yawned. I sniffed the air. I looked to see what the stuff was in the pocket in the car door and I found this book in there.

It must have been one of the books I'd boxed up for the charity shop. I had no idea how it'd got into the door pocket; it must have fallen out of the box. Maybe the mechanic who'd just looked the car over had found it under a seat and put it in there. Selected Herrick. It was a book I didn't remember at all. Was it even mine? When I opened it, it was full of notes in my writing, the writing of my much younger self, so I must've read it at some point.

My younger writing is narrow and pinched. My name, which I'd written on the first page, is squeezed up against itself as if determined to take up as little room as possible. I'd written things in pencil in the margins. *Carpe diem. Greek mythological nymphs who took care of beautiful garden.* On the inside back page I'd made a list of words I clearly thought were of use, *bunch assortment tussock shock sheaf truss heap swathe bouquet nosegay posy skein hank.* In the poems, I had underlined things; the phrase wild civility, the words and every tree / Now swaggers in her leafy gallantry.

Leafy gallantry. The words filled me with unease. Then they made me think of flowers in among, of all things, lightbulbs, batteries, hairdryers, curling tongs, irons, the stuff my father used to sell in his shop.

I laughed out loud, I laughed so loud that the person in the Audi in front of me reached to adjust his or her mirror to get a look at where the laughter was coming from.

It's over two decades, a quarter of a century ago, the day the child with the flowers came into my father's shop.

I was looking after the shop for my father while I was home on holiday. I was doing this for almost no salary because three electrical goods chainstores had recently come to our town. This meant people didn't bother bringing things in for repair because it was equally as cheap to throw things away and buy new ones outright (except not from my father's shop). Christmas was the time of year my father usually made most in the shop. This most recent Christmas he'd barely scraped through. One of the new chainstores was twenty yards from the front door of the shop and lit up like Christmas all the year round.

Now, though, it was Easter. I sat on the old kitchen stool at the counter every day that Easter holiday and read books for my Finals. It was literally quieter in there than a library. I picked at the sellotape over the rip in the cushioned seat of the stool and turned the page and the next page and nobody came in to buy anything.

The book I was reading was about the life of a poet. There wasn't much known about this poet's actual life, the book said, other than that his father killed himself by jumping out of a fourth-floor window, so the book was a lot about what it was like to be on the edge of poverty in the sixteenth and seventeenth centuries in the part of London called Cheapside, and about how the houses jutted out from themselves above their first floors, overhung themselves like mushrooms, or galleons, and how until 1661 the people in London had been duty-bound to see to the lighting of their own streets, required by law to hang out lit candles on dark nights. There were seventeenth-century line drawings of places called Fynnesburrie Field and Moor Field, great grassy flat expanses with a few peasants selling things drawn on them, drawings of women drying clothes flat on the grass, soldiers practising archery. The shop door opened and I looked up. A child came in, nine or ten, arms full of bluebells and primroses and sticking up in the air high above the child's head like radio aerials or butterfly antennae a couple of broken branches covered in blossom.

The child's long dark hair was girl-length and wavy, held back from falling across the eyes by two hairclips, one on each side of the head above the ears. Hairclips equalled girl. But it was something about the hairclips being so plain and then the face, a different kind of beautiful between them, that made me suspect that the child maybe wasn't what I'd first thought.

Where'd you get your flowers? I said.

Canal banks, the child said.

Up the canal was where the rougher girls at school tended to go to have sex with people. It was illicit no matter what you did up there. As children we weren't, ever, supposed to go up there. *Swear on your mother's life you won't grass about where we were.* So the child was suspect as soon as I heard the word canal.

It was true that the canal banks were often lined with bluebells at that time of year. But the branches, more likely they'd been snapped off trees like the ones in the front gardens of the houses in the Crown where the people who had money lived, closer to the town, far from the canal. I myself had grown up very close to the canal, which meant that anyone I told my address, if they knew the town at all, would be able to decide what sort of person I was and what kind of people my parents were – just like I was deciding stuff about this child, because something about him made me think of the woman who pushed the pram full of rags through the long grass of the fields at the backs of the houses, to whom my mother was always exceptionally polite and kind when this woman knocked on our door, and for whom she always saved our old clothes, done things, folded neatly in the cupboard at the back door where we kept the old newspapers.

It was with one of the twigs, with its roughly split greenwood end rather than its bud end, that the child pointed at the row of toasters in boxes on the shelf behind me – as if pointing the broken stick back not at the toasters at all but at himself.

That one please, he said.

I closed my book. I looked up at the toasters.

This one? I said.

The one next to it please, the child said.

That one's exactly the same as this one, I said.

It isn't, the child said.

They're all exactly the same, I said. It makes no difference which one I get down.

They look the same. But they are different

individual toasters of the same make and model, the child said.

It was true. I couldn't deny it. I grew haughty.

Pff, I said.

I climbed up two steps of the stepladder and picked up the first box I came to. I got down off the stepladder, put the box on the counter and told the child the price.

The child put the long twigs down on the counter next to the box and began peeling bluebell stems free of each other and laying the flowers separately out in front of me.

Is ten enough? the child said.

What for? I said.

The toaster, he said.

You're joking, I said.

How many do you need? the child said.

I pointed to the price sticker on the box. Then I picked up the box as if to put it back on the shelf. But the child looked panicked. So instead, with the toaster box under my arm, I came round the side of the counter and out into the front of the shop because it had struck me that maybe that child had pocketed something while I'd been up on the stepladder with my back turned.

But the child had no bag and only the thinnest grass-stained tee-shirt and shorts on, so I pretended to have gone out there especially to tidy the top layer of the rack of battery-powered mini-fans with the picture of the ecstatic woman cooling herself, a blur of little fan blades close to her delighted face. Not that anyone was ever likely to buy a mini-fan from an Inverness shop. The very existence of such an appliance was like a kind of highland Scottish joke. My father, an optimistic man, had ordered in fifty of them a couple of years ago plus this large display rack. Nobody had bought a single one.

Meanwhile the child, who was nearly as thin as those broken-off branches, as thin and sharp as a sapling whip, and whose eyebrows, as I saw when I came back round to my side of the counter, were low and troubled, was passing a single many-headed cowslip from one hand to the other.

Okay, this one too, he said putting the cowslip beside the other flowers next to the toaster.

You can't buy a toaster with these flowers, I said.

Which flowers *can* I buy it with? the child said.

If you want this toaster I'll need actual money, I said.

The child pointed again at the row of boxes above me.

That one instead? he asked.

This is a shop, I said.

Please? he said.

Don't be stupid, I said.

The child sighed. He looked me straight in the eye and dropped all his flowers out of his arms on to the counter. They lay there in a heap next to the petalled twigs and the toaster in its box. I shook my head.

No, I said.

I don't remember what happened next. I don't remember the child leaving. I presume he gathered up his flowers and left. Now, all the years later, I can't remember for the life of me the price of those toasters. What I can remember is the bruised look of the bluebells, the green of their stems against their own blueness next to the photo of the toaster on the side of the box. I remember the way the blossom on those flowering branches on the counter was giving way to the green of the leaves behind it.

The other thing I remember is that a month or so after that child came into the shop and tried to buy the toaster with sticks and bluebells, I was sitting an exam. It will have been a May morning, dust-motes lazy in the air in the sunlight above us coming through the high glass in the senate hall. I wrote down a quote from the poet I was answering on. As I did so I was filled with shame. Shame filled me literally, as if I were a jug held under a cold water tap.

The question was something about gallantry.

I bowed my head in the exam room with all the other heads bent over their papers in front of me, round me and behind me, all of us answering questions about poetry, and I felt like I had been found out. But about what, exactly, or what exactly it was I'd done to feel like that, I hadn't a clue.

A toaster.

A cowslip.

It makes me laugh now, sitting on the verge along from my still-ticking car, so long after. It makes me fond of my much younger self. I was moral, me, then. Decades it's taken me, finally to understand why I felt shame that May morning.

Here's one of the poems Robert Herrick wrote; it's called Upon a Child: An Epitaph.

> But born and, like a short delight,
> I glided past my parents' sight.
> That done, the harder Fates denied
> My longer stay, and so I died.
> If, pitying my sad parents' tears,
> You'll spill a tear or two with theirs,
> And with some flowers my grave bestrew,
> Love and they'll thank you for it. Adieu.

He was born in 1591 and died in 1674. When he was an infant, it says in the introduction, which I've been reading sitting here in this long grass with the May cold coming through my clothes, his father, Nicholas, either threw himself out of or fell out of the fourth-floor window of the house they lived in, leaving his widow not just with six children to feed, of whom the youngest was Robert the poet, but also pregnant with the seventh. Robert Herrick himself was apprenticed young to his uncle, a goldsmith, then went on to become a churchman. He is most famous, it says here, for his poems about girls, love, spring, flowers. Fair daffodils, we weep to see / ye haste away so soon. Then, then, methinks, how sweetly flows / That liquefaction of her clothes. How Roses Came Red. To a Bed of Tulips. To Violets. To Meadows. To Primroses Filled with Morning Dew. To Daisies, Not to Shut so Soon.

The car door is hanging open, the car parked as far up the verge as I can get it, but there's nobody on this road but me, there's been nobody for the last half hour. It's a while since I got out of the traffic and followed my nose through a couple of rough-looking villages whose high streets were boarded-up shops, past some well-to-do houses and barn conversions; I have no idea where I am right now but there are five or six different kinds of long grass here where I'm sitting. They must be different kinds because they have different shaped seed-heads. This one has a smooth stalk, dark green, and a head with long branching clumps of flowering seed on it. This one's seeds are much smaller and bushier. Its stalk is much lighter green. The core of the second one is sweeter, when I put it in my mouth, than the first.

I have no idea what the grasses are called. I recognize some of the flowers. That's ragwort. Those are cornflowers. That's red clover. Those are ox-eye daisies.

Swear on your mother's life. Nearly three decades on and my mother is dead, my father too. The place where the shop was is still there, though now it's a place selling highland clan souvenirs. That old woman who used to wheel the pram of rags; she must be long dead too.

I'd cover them with flowers. My mother, folding done things into neat piles for a poor woman; my father, imagining heatwaves for the Highlands: I'd gather up all the seasonals, the wild and the cut and the cultivated, the old roses, the new, the bluebells and primroses, the columbines and woodbines, the meadow cranesbill, the ragged robin, the jasmine, the honeysuckle, the poppies and cornflowers, the everything else, yellow cowslips, the cowslips particularly. I'd knock on the door of the house I grew up in and when they answered, my much younger parents, I'd cover the step with the wealth of them, and when that old woman knocked on the door with her rag pram I'd fill it till they came over the sides and filled the torn black hood, spilling on to the pavement behind her as she wheeled it off down the road.

I empty the change from my pockets into the long grass. The money disappears as I watch. I can still just see the edge of the fifty pence piece, so I pick it up again, turn it over, tails, heads, and check the date. 1997. It was a year I lived through. Britannia is sitting on a lion's flank holding a sprig in her hand. Olive? Laurel? I stand up. I throw the coin as far as I can into the thick new growth in the coppiced wood behind me.

Ha! It goes quite far.

I'd fill every toaster that ever stopped working, got thrown out, got buried in landfill. I'd fill all their slots with wild colours and flowerheads. I'd fill that old shop with the smell of this earth.

Here's what Helen Oyeyemi told me about the connective network of public libraries:

> *Public libraries were the making of me. The local library was a very practical solution to restlessness of mind plus very minimal funds. But the amazing thing was that there were three libraries in one. I lived close to the smallest of those (Deptford branch) but if I needed a book that the Deptford library didn't have, I was referred to the medium-sized library (Lewisham), which was a longer bus ride away, and if the medium-sized library didn't have the books I needed, then the biggest one definitely did, and I'd go all the way to Catford for those books. Between them these three never let me down. It was like*

living in a triangle of protection. The public library network definitely strikes me as some sort of live and benevolent organism.

Say I won't be there

I had a dream, I say.

Don't tell me about any dream right now, you say, I can't listen to it right now.

We are sitting in what characterizes weekday breakfast, which means us not saying anything and the Today programme on in the background. Today the Today programme is about the possible break-up of the Eurozone, about a government scheme to give parents online training in how to look after new babies, and about how some government people are swearing they're not in the pockets of newspaper people regardless of any SMS messages they may have sent to them and how nobody is going to resign. The word they keep using is transparent.

It's not just any dream, it's the recurring dream, I

say. The one I've been having all year. I had it again. I keep having it.

Tautology, you say.

What? I say.

You just said the same thing four times over, you say. And I can't hear about your dream right now. I've got work in a minute.

I've got work too, I say.

Then I don't say anything for a minute because we both know that sending CVs out online to try and find work doesn't really constitute work.

Anyway I don't want to tell you it, I say. I'm just telling you the fact that I had it again.

Good, you say.

There's a graveyard in it, I say.

In the dream? you say.

You raise your head from your coffee because today the company you work for is meeting some people who run a business which is extending its premises into the site of an old churchyard, to see if the people like the company's plans for turning burial ground into tidy new landscaping. Some of the things I've said to you about this and that you've shrugged your shoulders at are: *are you allowed to do that?* and *what about the dead people?* and *you can't tidy a graveyard into something else, it's always going to be a graveyard.* If the graveyard deal falls through it looks like your job will too, because your company is laying off people right left and centre.

Am I in it? you say.

The graveyard? I say.

The dream, you say. Don't tell me the whole dream. I just want to know if I'm in it.

You're not, I say, and it's not your graveyard, it's a 1960s graveyard. And I'm not even in the dream, myself. I mean, I'm *in* it, but not as me.

How then? you say.

Well, I say, in it I'm a different person. I'm, like, a character in a 1960s novel.

Which 1960s novel? you say. Who by?

Not a real actual novel, I say. Not a novel that exists. I'm just trying to find a way to describe what it feels like to have the dream.

And you're *like* a character or you *are* a character? you say.

Pedant, I say.

Are there scooters? you say.

Eh? I say.

Milk machines? you say. Where you put your coin in and a little carton of milk drops out. Photo booths. Record booths, upstairs in Woolworths. Where you wait your turn then you listen to a record and don't have to buy it.

Don't start trying to turn my dream into a cheap graphic-designy version of the 1960s, I say.

Are there any women in it who are pregnant and

thinking about having an abortion but know how impossible that'll be so they end up having a terrible miscarriage because they have to go to a backstreet place to have it done? you say.

Yes, hundreds of them, I say, and they're all queuing up looking aggrieved at the future. Stop hijacking my dream.

How do you know it's a 1960s *book* and not a 1960s *film*? you say.

I'm not telling any pedant anything else about any dream of mine, I say.

I told you already I don't want to hear about your stupid dream – you say.

It's not a stupid dream – I say.

And I was just interested for a moment in the form it's taking, you say. Because dreams are usually really visual, aren't they? More like films. Is it like A Hard Day's Night?

No, I say.

Do you remember that time we were driving back from Wales, you say, and I was falling asleep at the wheel and the only way we could keep me awake was to play the soundtrack of A Hard Day's Night really loud?

No, I say.

No? you say.

No I don't, I say. And it's not like a film, it's grimier, and calmer, and smaller, and less meaningful than a film is. It's kind of nothing. And everything.

How does that make it a novel? you say.

It's like I can sort of taste the paper, I say, and smell it, the paper the book's made with, even though I'm sort of seeing it happen.

Seeing what? you say.

There's this man with his arm in a sling, I say, and he comes home from work late one night and goes up the stairs and there are these three small girls all in a row in a bed, tucked in, they're asleep, but he wakes them. So he can tell them.

Tell them what? you say.

I thought you didn't want me to tell you my dream, I say.

I've got to go in a minute, you say. Come on.

He tells them, I say, how the day before he comes home – he's been down south working in London – anyway the day before, he's just walking along the road, turning a corner on an ordinary London street on his way to work when all of a sudden he sees her.

Who? you say.

Dusty Springfield, I say.

Dusty? you say. Really? What's she singing?

She isn't singing anything, I say, she's having her photograph taken in a graveyard by a man from the Daily Mirror.

How do you know he's from the Daily Mirror? you say.

I just do, I say. Dream logic.

I can't believe she's not singing something, you say. That's because you don't like her music.

I do so like her music, I say. I just don't know very much about it.

You don't even know a single song she sang, you say.

I do so, I say.

Name some songs, you say.

She sings the song in that Quentin Tarantino film where the man gets his ear cut off, I say.

Son of a Preacher Man, you say, and it's not in that film, it's in a different Tarantino film.

Whatever, I say.

Name one, you say. Just one.

That one where she waves her arms about in the air when she sings it, I say. And that song about only wanting to be with you, that Annie Lennox sang. And, uh, she sings, eh, she also –

It's me who likes Dusty, not you, you say. And you've stolen my workplace too. Dusty Springfield. In the graveyard. Your dream is filched from me. You've taken something I like and you've put it into something I'm working on. You're filching my subconscious.

No I'm not, I say. I've been having this dream much longer than you've been working on any graveyard project. I've been having this dream for more than a year.

Well, where's it come from? you say. It must have come from somewhere. Is it something that happened in your childhood?

No, I say. Not at all.

Is it your father in the dream? Did your father do something like that? Who are the other two girls in the bed? Is it from before your mother went?

All the people in the dream, I say, are strangers to me. I recognize them, but only from having dreamed about them before. And I'm looking out of the eyes of a different person in the dream every time I dream it.

You're looking at the clock. You stand up, wipe the crumbs from round your mouth, wash your hands at the sink and take your ironed shirt off the back of the spare chair. I follow you to the hall mirror.

So sometimes I'm the man coming up the stairs, I say, and sometimes I'm the girls' mother, and sometimes I'm one or other of the three girls in the bed.

You are buttoning yourself up.

And sometimes you're Dusty? you say.

No, I say. I never get to be Dusty. Not yet, anyway.

Why? you say.

I don't think we get to choose with dreams, I say. And properly speaking, she isn't actually in the dream. I never get to *see* her. I only get to hear about her or tell people about seeing her.

You are at the door now pulling your jacket on. Your ironed shirt is rumpling up already beneath the jacket.

Right then. Bye then. Wish me luck, you say.

Luck, I say.

See you later. I'll text you, you say.

Not if I text you first, I say.

The door shuts behind you.

I go back and sit at the table in the noise of the radio news.

The people on the radio tell me that the jobless figures are down, but that if you look at the statistic while taking other statistics into account the jobless figures are up. A presenter tells me I can send in my thoughts. He tells me the hashtag. He tells me about the 24 hour newsfeeds online and how to contact the programme. It is amazing how many ways there are now to be personally in touch with what's happening in the world. The presenter reads out a couple of comments some people have emailed or tweeted.

I look at the shut door. Houses change when people come in and out of them. Even the radio sounds different with just me here; this whole house and all the air in it is practically reeling with your going, even though it's just a simple going, an everyday off-to-work kind of going.

I am far too sensitive. Something will have to be done about such sensitivity.

There was a time in our lives, some years ago now, when you and I took to writing down our dreams. It was when we were still being idealistic about our relationship. We wanted to see how dreams would read, especially after time had passed and immediacy had blurred. We wanted to see if two different people's dreams could have anything in common. I remember us arranging, some nights, before we went to sleep, to meet in our dreams. Of course, we never did. You can't control dreams. And partly we started writing them down – though we didn't say so out loud – because it's really boring to have to sit and listen, in the morning when you're hardly awake yourself, to a dream someone else has had, which inevitably sounds mad because dreams always sound mad, and can go on for what seems like ever.

We bought the book in Habitat, before Habitat became defunct. We wrote dreams down in it for about six months, this is eight or nine years ago now. It's a blank book with thick hand-made paper and hand-stitching up the spine; its cover has an Indian goddess riding an elephant on it in a kind of Bollywood poster image. It's underneath the couch in the front room, quarter-filled with outdated dreams. At least I'm assuming it's under the couch. We tend to dislodge it yearly when summer comes around and we pull the deckchair out and find it again among the long sashes of dust that have formed themselves of what's escaped the hoover since the end of the summer before.

*

At lunchtime you send me a text. It arrives at exactly the same time as an email from you in my inbox. The text is quite long. Before I have time to read either, the doorbell goes. I answer the door and a girl courier, holding her bike by the handlebars, gives me a padded envelope. While I'm signing the form on her clipboard, the house phone kicks into answerphone behind me and I can hear your voice leaving a message. When I get back into the kitchen there's also a voicemail from you waiting on my mobile. I look at the envelope in my hand. My name and the address on it are in your writing.

I press the button on the house answerphone first, since your voice was in the room just a moment ago. The automaton tells me the date and the day and the time. Then you. *Hi. I just wanted to inform your subconscious that one day in the 1960s Dusty Springfield was eating in the revolving restaurant at the top of the new Post Office Tower. And she saw a head waiter giving a lower ranking waiter a hard time, the head waiter was tearing a strip off him about something, and Dusty Springfield thought the telling-off was unjustified, so she picked up a bread roll from a basket on the table and she threw it at that head waiter and hit him with it. Bye for now. Love.*

Then your message ends, the automaton voice repeats the time it got recorded, and the recorder rewinds and switches itself off.

I pick up my mobile and press the text icon. This is what your text says. *In 1964 Dusty Springfield was kept under house arrest in a South African hotel for several days because she refused to play a concert where the venue was racially segregated. This got her into considerable trouble not just in South Africa but at home too where other entertainers, among them contemporary luminaries like Max Bygraves and Derek Nimmo, complained to the papers that by doing this she was endangering their chances of performing in South Africa.* xxx

Your email, by comparison, is very short. *Dusty Springfield was 1 of the reasons in the 1960s that Motown music reached the UK at all* xxx

I press the voicemail button on my mobile. *Hi. It's me. I just wanted to let your subconscious know that at the end of the 60s, well, in 1970, Dusty Springfield told a newspaper that she was every bit as capable of being swayed, in terms of sexual attraction, by a girl as by a boy. At the time this was as you might imagine a near-incendiary thing for anyone to say out loud, even though male homosexuality had (though only very recently) been decriminalized. In England, not in Scotland. In Scotland it wasn't legal till 1980. Love. See you later. Bye.*

The only message left now is whatever's in the padded envelope. I open it.

Inside is a bright orange CD box with two men and a woman in what look like 50s clothes on the cover. Did the early 60s really look so like the 50s? The men are both looking straight at the camera and holding guitars. The woman, a very early Dusty Springfield, is clasping her hands and looking upwards, demure, like a good girl, well, I say girl, but she looks like she could be any age between fifteen and fifty.

There's a note in the padded envelope. I unfold it. In your handwriting, it says *Hi. This is a present for your thief of a subconscious from the early 1960s. The song called Island of Dreams stayed in the charts for the whole first half of 1963. It has a Thomas Hardy reference in it which I thought you'd enjoy. If I'm remembering rightly Dusty Springfield was unhappy with her vocal on this song, she thought it was too nasal and slightly off key, but then she was the kind of perfectionist who, after she went solo that same year, would do things like insist on recording her vocals in the echo of the ladies toilets or the stairwells of the Philips Music building, to get the tonal dimension she particularly wanted.*

I sit at the table. I shake my head. I start writing a text. Thank you for the lectures in 1960s memorabilia. Did you get the job. Did you not get the job. Love.

But then instead of sending it, I delete it. I put the phone down on the table and open the CD box.

The song called Island of Dreams begins with a melancholy harmonica wail. Then a lopey rhythm sets in, swings along in an almost country and western way into a song about someone who can't forget, and what she can't forget is a lovely love affair which took place on a beautiful island, the island of dreams. High in the sky is a bird on the wing. Please carry me with you. Far far away from the mad rushing crowd. Please carry me with you.

I spend the rest of the afternoon listening to the two CDs of digitally remastered songs by The Springfields. Far Away Places With Strange Sounding Names. Say I Won't Be There. Where Have All The Flowers Gone? (Sag Mir, Wo Die Blumen Sind). The last of these is sung in English and German by The Springfields, not very long after the war. The songs have an innocent bravado about them. Several songs slip not just from one language to another but from one national musical style to another, a bluntly international noise, raucous then soothing then raucous again sometimes in the same song. At the centre of all of them there's this female vocal, tough and delicate, sometimes both in the space of a single held note.

I'm surprised by how many of the songs I know. I'm almost embarrassed by their sheer energy, their optimism. It makes me think of the front garden of the new council house, churned-up waist-high mud when my parents arrived, all roses by the time I was small, and of one of my few memories of my mother, the day she ran down the road with a shovel after the milkman's horse and cart had clopped past and the horse had left balls of dung on the tarmac steaming in the cold of April, my mother coming back with it and digging the bright smell of horseshit in round the roots of the bushes.

*

I'll write a book instead, you say. I'll call it The Dream: Grime and Transcendence In The 1960s Novel.

Not very catchy title, I say. It'll need to be better.

We're in bed. It's later. We've been out for supper, to spend money while we have it and to talk about ways we might be able to make it when we need to, urgently, again, quite soon. That conversation didn't last long. But now the very nice wine is wearing off. We're lying beside each other, both with our arms behind our heads, both looking at the ceiling of our house. Not our house. The house belongs to the bank. The bank belongs to a different planet, aeons away from the planet which the people who have to use the banks live on. So much for space travel.

Ah, it was all about things being better, getting better, back then, you say.

Grime was transcendent back then, I say.

Hems were transcendent back then, you say.

Everything was transcendent back then, I say.

We'll be all right, you say.

Course we will, I say. We'll transcend.

It's not the transc-end of the world, you say.

It never is, I say. Listen. I was wondering. Is Dusty Springfield actually dead?

No, Dusty will never die, you say. She died in the late nineties I think.

Where's she buried? I say.

In your dream, you say.

She's not buried in my dream, I say.

Don't tell me your dream, you say.

She's having her picture taken in my dream, I say.

Yeah, and now you're so fully prepared, you'll *really* see her next time you dream that dream, you say.

In fact, I say, she's not actually having her picture taken in my dream. She's just a character in a story told by someone else.

Very postmodern structure, you say. Grime and transcendence in the postmodern 1960s novel. Don't tell me it.

I'll never ever tell you it, I say, and nothing you can do will ever make me.

I don't know if she even *is* buried, you say. She might be scattered. It'll probably say on Wiki.

So much information so little time, I say.

Scattered, spore-like, broken down and molecular, the hopes and the dreams and the new wipe-clean linoleums, you say. The new exciting fabrics and the clothes made of paper, the moisture from the evaporated coffee-bar steam of a recovering nation. Scattered, the notes of all the sung songs. Scattered, the filaments of light of all the new mornings that dawned across the brand new motorways with hardly any cars on them, the fogs and the smogs dispersing, the flashing neons dimming in the dawn light, season after season, round Eros in Piccadilly. There. That's your opening page.

Eros isn't scattered, I say. He's still there. I saw him, for real, last week, in London.

You saw Eros? you say. For real?

Well, the statue, I say. Not your actual Eros.

If you ever see my actual Eros –, you say. In a dream, say.

Uh huh? I say.

Whatever you do –, you say.

I won't tell you, I say.

*

The father shakes us awake. He's sitting on the end of the bed in the light from the landing; the bedroom door's open and the mother's coming up the stairs saying don't wake them, don't, Fred, it's late.

This time in the dream I am the one in the middle of the bed, the smallest. I've had the flu. Because I'm still not quite better from the flu, I've been put to bed earliest, and before my sisters got put to bed too, right at the beginning of the dream, I leaned on our windowsill with the vintage car models my mother bought me because I had the flu, and raced them along the length of the sill. There was ice on the inside rim of the window. When I put my tongue on it, it tasted of the metal of the window frame. The vintage car toys are beautiful. I know the other two sisters are already thinking about how to steal them. But for the moment in the dream they're mine.

The father smells of alcohol. His arm is in a sling. The eldest of the sisters asks him how he did it.

He did it in a pub fight, the mother says at the door.

The father talks over the top of her.

Guess who I saw, he says. Yesterday morning, early in the morning. I was walking down the street between the bus stop and work and I turned a corner, and guess who I saw, in person, in the flesh. Dusty Springfield.

Both the sisters get very excited. I am too sleepy

to be excited, and I am not completely sure who Dusty Springfield is.

The sister who sleeps on the wall side of the bed writes secret poems in the spare pages in the back of the pocket dictionary she has for school. One of the poems is about how it would feel to be a vagrant or a beggar. She always gives any pocket money she might have to the people, if she's passing them, who came back from the war with one leg or one arm missing and sit on the pavements outside the big shops.

(When I'm this sister in the dream I know that she believes that the singer Dusty Springfield, who was New Musical Express's most popular female vocalist again last year, would understand what it is like to be her.)

The sister on the door side of the bed is good at everything. A photo has been taken of her in her school uniform sitting at her desk pretending to write things down. It is framed on the sideboard downstairs.

(When I'm this sister in the dream I know that she has noticed that the singer Dusty Springfield, whose eyes look as black as the vinyl of her 45s, uses her eyeshadow like a mask with which she protects herself.)

Dusty Springfield! the mother is saying. She looks in awe in the landing light. She comes and sits on the end of the bed beside the father.

(When I'm her in the dream and she says this, I can feel her heart open wider, like an eye inside her.)

She was having her photograph taken, the father says. And I thought to myself, wait till I tell my girls.

(When I'm him in the dream I know, as he throws himself and his story headlong up the stairs, how full his own heart is with bringing home the story.)

And there were a lot of people there from the Daily Mirror, he says, a photographer and people, and there must have been lights, because the graveyard was lit up and she was standing way back in among all these old graves and overgrown grass and plants and suchlike, and she was wearing a bright pink suit, bright pink trousers and a bright pink jacket with her hair all yellow and up like it is, and she had her arms out like this.

The father flings his one arm that's not in a sling out wide. At the same time, because he's forgotten, he tries to fling the arm in the sling out too.

Ouch! he says like it really hurt to, then the mother starts to laugh, then he laughs too.

And that, each time, is where the dream ends and I wake up.

Anna James put it like this:

> *Public libraries were hugely important to me growing up, as we lived in a fairly small village on the outskirts of Newcastle with minimal sources of entertainment. Without access to that library, as small and stern as it was, I don't think I would be the reader I am now. That tiny library gave me access to worlds and lives that a child growing up in rural Northumberland could never have hoped to experience anywhere else. And so when I left university becoming a school librarian was the obvious choice for me, and I spent nearly five years working with 11–18-year-olds in Coventry, trying to give them that same access to the infinite possibilities of libraries.*

This is what Richard Popple said:

> *The spectre of library closures in the current financial climate of austerity is, to a limited extent, understandable. Of course councils are looking to save money where they can, and, while libraries do have several sources of income, they are not set up to be profit-making themselves. Libraries are, at heart, helpful and kind providers. It is hard for those who perhaps don't feel the need to visit their local libraries to understand what a vital service they provide for communities and individuals who do – and those who do are often the most vulnerable.*
>
> *Libraries provide free access to computers, and help with using them. This is so important as more and more services – job-searching, flight bookings, bus pass applications etc – now prefer or even require internet access. So for those who can't afford a computer and are trying to find a job, or for those who did not grow up with the technology, the free access to technology and human assistance is becoming increasingly essential. Libraries provide this for everyone.*
>
> *They also provide access to (generally free) entertainment and activities for children and adults. These can help individuals and communities not to be isolated.*
>
> *And – books! Free books! Entertainment,*

knowledge, ideas, imagination, and all with the liberty to try book after book at no cost. And even if you're housebound and unable to get to the library, they'll usually have a service to choose and bring the books for you.

It is the poorest, most isolated and the least able in our society who suffer most if they are gone. So if our society does not care for libraries, then it is not caring for its most vulnerable.

Tracy Bohan told me a little of what's happening to the public library in her neighbourhood:

The council intend to offer it up to developers and presumably just go with the highest bid. It will undoubtedly become flats. The council has also cut the 2016 park budget in half. And they just razed an entire housing estate to make way for a private development.

And finally, Sarah Wood told me this:

After my mother died, I was clearing out the little compartments in her purse – the reward cards, credit cards, driving licence, they'd all become meaningless. The one thing I couldn't bring myself to throw away was her library card.

And so on

Every time I sit down to try to write this story – which is a commission for a short story anthology where all the stories have to be about death – life intervenes.

What I mean is, I have a friend who died far too young. In one of the fevers she was in, in hospital, she thought she was being abducted by art thieves. She believed that what was happening to her wasn't that she was so ill she was hallucinating, but that she was a work of art and she was being stolen by unscrupulous people.

When she was recovering – before she caught an infection, became gravely ill all over again then, weak from having been ill for so long, died – she sent me a very funny text about thinking she was art and was being stolen and how deluded she'd been. She couldn't eat or drink at this point but she could send texts. The texts were very much in her voice, and now that she's dead I hear that voice in my ear a lot, *what about you?* that was her way of saying hello; she was Irish; and more and more I'm coming to understand that she *was* a work of art and that she has, after all, been stolen by art thieves who are keeping her hidden until they can work out how to make a fortune from her, or maybe they already have, maybe she's been sold already to a massively rich art collector who keeps her out of the public eye, shows her only to a select number of extremely rich and equally unscrupulous colleagues.

That art collector's lucky to be anywhere near my friend. My stolen friend will enhance that collector's life. She will also alter his or her library shelves for the better; she will add a stack of bent old paperbacks, so well read that they barrel like accordions, to the shelves of stolen first editions and filched rare texts; she will add books by people that that collector's never thought to read. She will fill the collector's house with unimagined resonances, unexpected mythological, cultural, ancient and contemporary information and understanding, about which she was a walking library of rare things herself. She'll change that person's heart, whoever stole her, so that simply by dint of being in her presence he or she will soon be showing all the dodgily come-by artworks in the palazzo or mansion or wherever the collector lives to the public for free, and letting homeless people sleep in the forty-nine extra rooms that nobody else uses in that house – even sleep at the foot of his or her own bed.

Or if she's been filched by amateurs, then right now somewhere in Europe an old woman is swearing to the prosecutor that she never saw her son do anything wrong, she knows he hasn't, she'll swear on her life he hasn't, he never brought home anything or anyone untoward, and that those long rolled-up canvas things she burned in the brazier weren't precious original artworks at all – and all the time she'll be longing to get out of the police station and home again simply to sit by the empty brazier with my dead friend who, having saved the da Vincis and Matisses and Cézannes and Munchs from any such fate by persuading her not to burn them, is sitting alongside her and distracting her with story after story, stories maybe a bit like this one:

listen to this, an old woman who's been fighting with all her closest relatives almost all her life, in fact hasn't spoken to or had any contact with any of them for more than a decade, goes to the doctor and finds out she's got terminal something. She comes home from the doctor's and she's troubled. Not about her death, she doesn't think about that for a moment, she doesn't give a toss about dying – except when it comes to who's going to inherit her considerable wealth and belongings and estate. More than anything she wants to make sure none of what's hers is going to go to any relatives she particularly dislikes.

The thing is, she can't remember which of them it is she dislikes most. Or least. She decides to choose one of them and leave it all as incontestably as possible to the person of her choice. But which one?

So she writes and invites all five of her relatives to come and stay with her for a week. In that week, she thinks, she'll be able to sort wheat from chaff. Because they all know she's quite rich, and because they guess she might be dying, her relatives all write back immediately saying they've accepted her invitation and her offer of free plane tickets (they live in America or Australia, somewhere far away). The day approaches and she's got everything ready for them, all the beds made up, all the food in the fridge. They arrive safely. One of them phones her from the airport to tell her they'll be with her in a couple of hours.

Then the taxi they're in on the way to her house crashes on the motorway and they're all killed.

The old woman is more annoyed about her plan being ruined than that they're dead. She arranges for a group funeral for them and doesn't attend it. The week after that, she advertises in the papers and online for five actors. One of the conditions is that applicants must be able to sacrifice their Christmas holidays.

She turns on the radiators in the front room of her house and holds the auditions there. She provides each person auditioning with a list of attributes and characteristics. She chooses the five she imagines most resemble her dead family members.

Next, she hires a theatre director and tells him exactly what she wants the actors to do in the ten days they'll spend with her.

For a week the director schools the five actors she's chosen in the roles she's outlined.

On Christmas Eve the five actors move into her house with her. The heating stays on in the front room throughout. On 2 January she pays them handsomely as promised and waves them all out of her house.

She turns the radiators in the front room back to their off positions.

As she goes upstairs, her house feels cavernous. She realizes she's dying.

The doorbell rings when she's halfway up the stairs. Two of her actor family members are at the door. They'd got as far as the bus stop. They'd looked at each other and they'd turned back to the house.

One of them says that they'd noticed their aunt isn't keeping as well as she might.

They ask if they might move in with her.

In reality, it wasn't my friend who died young who told me that story. It was told to me by a different friend, still as alive as you and me (well, me right now). The postscript to her telling me was funny. My (live) friend had heard half this story on the radio, come in halfway through and heard it, and she had loved it, and had congratulated the writer Angela Huth (who's a friend of hers and who she thought she heard the announcer credit at the end) the next time she saw her at some function or other, on writing such a good story.

Thanks, but it wasn't me. I don't know that story. I didn't write it, Angela Huth said.

Ah well, my (live) friend said to me when she told me it, never mind whose story it is, I stole it off the radio and now I'm giving it to you.

And now I've passed it on to you, whoever you are, reading this story. We're all in receipt of stolen goods, which is probably the only conclusion I can draw in a story meant to be about death, a story which, when I sat down today to write it, I'd decided would be about the terrible beauty of a French woman dead in a ditch in 1940, after a German plane has sprayed a line of people walking along a tree-lined road trying to get away from bombardments in the city. I'd planned that it would be all about her, that this is what I'd write about, before my friends (dead and alive) intervened.

There she is, her coat flung open, her blouse still pristine, for five seconds or so, it's not long after her death, on an episode of The World At War playing yesterday lunchtime on BBC2 (you can see it on iPlayer catch-up for the next fifty-three days). I stole her – well, or borrowed her; I'd thought this might be a story about how beautiful she was, and about how the realizing of the fact of her beauty, as I watched the programme, filled me with disgust at my being able to see, and so effortlessly, not one, not two, not three, but five whole seconds of her life and her just-happened death in a way that was so far beyond that woman's power or choice – never mind my being able to have the luxury of any aesthetic response. Most obscene, though, is the knowledge that there *was* a future, and that I, or anyone, could so casually inhabit it after such a thing happening even to just one person of all the millions and millions and millions and so on whose ends were futile and foul in a war several wars back, seventy-five years ago.

And since we're talking violent unfair death: is it easier to feel fury and hurt, or simply just to feel, about something like that woman's death so long ago, than it is when it comes to the ubiquity of deaths, deaths on deaths, in the world in all the papers and on all the news sites right now in the form of the most up to date of our dead: a pilot burned alive, a poet shot by the police in the square where she was laying memorial flowers, the journalists and the aid workers filmed in the act of their dying, the students, the townfuls of kidnapped and casually executed people, all the hundreds of stolen lives just over the past ten days – and those are only the ones we know about?

What about you? There's my dead friend again, nudging my arm. Hello. Yesterday, after I saw that episode of World At War, I was on a train reading in the paper all about the latest deaths and thinking how I'd like to kill the man behind me who kept coughing in that way that meant that probably he'd got a contagious cold and that my chair jolted every time he coughed since he had long legs, he was too big for the train seats, his knees were jammed up the back of my seat. To stop myself minding, I played the game on my phone, the one where you cancel all the dots of the same colour to win points, Two Dots, which ought to be called Thanatos, not Two Dots, being the perfect example of the stasis at the heart of the death-drive –

which reminds me. Here's a story about death, etc. I once went to Greece with a friend (I don't know whether this friend's alive or dead. I could look on Facebook to try and find out – though there's a chance I'd still be none the wiser since so many people on Facebook who are in reality dead still get happy birthday wishes year in year out from automated Friends on their automated birthdays). We stayed in a tiny village a couple of miles inland on an island, and on the second day there, having failed to find our way to a beach or even just to the sea, we started asking locals to point us in the right direction. It was a tiny island, a place there weren't many other tourists, and no one we met in the street spoke English. My friend could speak a little Greek. But people kept treating us strangely. One woman took us to a church; it was very beautiful, full of freesias for Easter. An old man put his hand on my friend's arm. He looked at us kindly, he patted us both on the back. By the end of the day the whole village was nodding at us as we passed, and people kept coming out of houses to give us gifts – halva; a picture of a saint with a blackbird bringing him things to eat; a collection of little tin rectangles, one with an eye imprinted in it, one with a heart, one with a leg.

At the airport in Athens, on our stop-off on the way home, the waitress who served us laughed out loud.

That's not the word for sea, she said. You've been asking people the way to death and demise.

Ha ha!

I wish I could tell my friend who died that story. But then, if she were still alive, I probably wouldn't think to, wouldn't want to in the same way. And in some ways here I am doing exactly that, telling all this in the direction of my friend who died young and was a work of art, no: a work of life, though she died so roughly, and wherever those thieves are hiding her till they can sell her, they have to tape blankets over the windows because the light coming off her mind, even though she's dead, gives away her whereabouts, and they have to keep pulling up and cutting back the flowers and tendrils and green stuff that persistently crack the stone of the floors of wherever they've got her. That's the art of dying all right.

Pretty soon that whole place will resemble I don't know what, probably a library, one with trees growing right through its floors up past its shelves and piercing its roof. They'll try and stop it happening; they'll move her to the next empty cave or mansion or cellar or wherever, but it doesn't matter where she is. She'll do the same to it and to the one after it and to the one after that, and so on.

Acknowledgements and grateful thanks to the following publications, where stories from this collection first appeared:
Ox-Tales Fire; *New Statesman*; *Goodbye to All That*; *Elsewhere*; *The Times*; *Harper's Bazaar*.
'The beholder' was originally commissioned by Durham Literature Festival and published, along with 'The poet', in *Shire* (2012). 'The definite article' was first published in the Park Stories series and is dedicated to Mary Chadwick.

Thank you to everyone
who helped in some way with this book,
by telling me or sending me their library stories.

Special thanks to Kate Atkinson, Lori Beck, Xandra Bingley, Tracy Bohan, Lesley Bryce, Mary Chadwick, Helen Clyne, Lucy Gulland, Alexandra Harris, Debbie Hodder, Pat Hunter, Anna James, Clare Jennings, Jackie Kay, Eve Lacey, Olivia Laing, Sophie Mayer, Cathy Moore, Helen Oyeyemi, Richard Popple, Simon Prosser, Anna Ridley, Kamila Shamsie, Miriam Toews, Miriam Toews's mother, Emily Wainwright, Natalie Williams, Emma Wilson, Sarah Wood.

ALSO BY

ALI SMITH

HOW TO BE BOTH

Passionate, compassionate, vitally inventive, and scrupulously playful, Ali Smith's novels are like nothing else. Borrowing from painting's fresco technique to make an original literary double-take, *How to be both* is a novel all about art's versatility. It's a fast-moving, genre-bending conversation between forms, times, truths, and fictions. There's a Renaissance artist of the 1460s. There's the child of a child of the 1960s. Two tales of love and injustice twist into a singular yarn where time gets timeless, knowing gets mysterious, fictional gets real—and all life's givens get given a second chance.

Fiction

ALSO AVAILABLE

The Accidental

The Book Lover

The First Person and Other Stories

Hotel World

There but for the

The Whole Story and Other Stories

ANCHOR BOOKS

Available wherever books are sold.

www.anchorbooks.com